"Did I ever ask you for anything... then?"

Jerard snorted contemptuously. "No. I *offered* it. I offered you marriage," he revealed bitterly.

"And I married Anthony." Velvet's mouth twisted. "So much for that theory, Mr. Daniels. Perhaps you can give it a little more thought and come up with the answer as to why I married Anthony, if it isn't already obvious enough." She paused. "I loved *him*. And whatever time I spent with you was just an impetuous interlude—and one I would rather forget had ever happened."

"I thought you already had," he scorned.

Her head was held high. "I have, but *you* haven't."

"And I don't ever intend to. It will serve to remind me of the deceit of women—something I'd forgotten by loving you." He turned his back on her.

CAROLE MORTIMER
is also the author of these

Harlequin Presents

Many of these titles are available at your local bookseller.

For a free catalog listing all titles currently available,
send your name and address to:

HARLEQUIN READER SERVICE,
1440 South Priest Drive, Tempe, AZ 85281
Canadian address: Stratford, Ontario N5A 6W2

CAROLE MORTIMER

forgotten lover

Harlequin Books

TORONTO • NEW YORK • LOS ANGELES • LONDON
AMSTERDAM • PARIS • SYDNEY • HAMBURG
STOCKHOLM • ATHENS • TOKYO • MILAN

For
John and Matthew

———————————◆———————————

Harlequin Presents first edition October 1982
ISBN 0-373-10539-8

Original hardcover edition published in 1982
by Mills & Boon Limited

. CHAPTER ONE

VELVET posed in front of the camera once again, her smile forced now as the sun continued to beat down on her, her make-up feeling as if it were streaking down her face. They had attracted quite a crowd of people as Paul set up his photographic equipment on the Fort Lauderdale beach, the holiday town twenty miles from Miami. Thank God they hadn't decided to film in Miami itself; the one day they had spent there the beach had been absolutely crowded.

As it was they had attracted quite a few people, most of them male, all watching with interest as she and Carly posed in the numerous beach outfits. The shorts were very brief, some of the sun-tops even briefer, and this was obviously appreciated by their onlookers.

But despite the briefness of their clothing it was still terribly hot, the temperature in the nineties, and only being used to the coolness of English weather this heat had come as something of a shock to Velvet. All she longed to do right now was strip off, don one of the numerous bikinis she had brought with her, and run across the golden-white sand and into the deep blue sea, its coolness refreshing and invigorating.

Fort Lauderdale certainly lived up to its reputation. The people were very friendly, the beaches unbelievable, even down to the palm trees that grew tall and straight even in the strong sea-breeze. The sand was fine and smooth down to the sea edge, the water still and calm, the waves lapping gently against the shoreline. Tall hotels, and one and two-storey motels edged the beach across the shore road, their walls freshly painted in gay attractive colours. It was in one of these hotels that the

7

three of them were staying, with a breathtaking view of the ocean from their rooms, both in the blazing sunlight hours and the bright moonlight.

But today was their first day of actually working, the previous day having been taken up in recovering from the nine-hour flight. Never having worked in such a climate before, Velvet hadn't been prepared for the overwhelming heat and humidity that seemed to hit her like a blanket as soon as she had stepped out of their air-conditioned hotel this morning. Her brief clothing had instantly seemed too heavy, her make-up feeling caked on to her face, and all her energy seemed to be stripped from her. And that was before she had even begun working!

The last hour had seemed like a lifetime, each change of clothes taking longer than the last, and her movements were now slow and sluggish.

She threw off the straw hat. 'No more, Paul,' she complained. 'I can't do any more today.' The blue sea behind her beckoned temptingly, increasingly so as each minute passed.

His camera lowered, his features boyishly youthful despite his thirty-two years, Paul was very slightly built, his blond hair over-long, his features striking rather than handsome. Because he spent so much time with women his manner was sometimes effeminate, often leading to snide remarks from people who envied him his skill with a camera, but Velvet knew that these remarks were unfounded. He and Carly, the other model on this assignment, had been living together for the past year.

'Just another couple of shots,' he encouraged. 'Then we can all stop for the day. Okay?'

'Okay,' she sighed her agreement, and donned the hat again, sure that by now she must look a mess and not the beautiful model she was supposed to be.

Carly looked up hopefully from her sitting position

on the sand. 'Does that mean I can go and get changed?'

'Yes, go,' Paul told her in a preoccupied voice.

She stood up, grimacing. 'So nice to be wanted!'

Paul ignored her, all his concentration on his camera and subject. He didn't even see the models who stood before him as women, they were merely objects that he wanted to show to advantage with his skill as a photographer. Velvet loved to be photographed by him, knew he would bring out the best in her. If he hadn't been the photographer on this assignment she doubted she would even have accepted it, hating having to leave Tony with her brother and his wife.

Not that Tony minded, he loved staying with his Uncle Simon and Aunty Janice. But Velvet herself felt guilty about leaving him, and would have brought him with her if it hadn't been such a long flight. As a working widow she took Tony with her as much as possible, possibly a little too possessive of him. But he was all she had left of her husband Anthony, her dearly loved Anthony who had died shortly after their marriage.

But Tony was all she could ever wish for in her child, full of energy, so much so that he tired her out just looking at him. He was a beautiful child, almost eighteen months of pure devilment, his huge innocent brown eyes totally deceptive, as were his cherubic features and baby blond curls. Oh, how she missed him already!

'There, finished,' Paul lowered his camera. 'You can go and get changed too.'

She wiped her damp face. 'I think I'll go back to the hotel and put on one of my own bikinis before I go in for a swim.'

'Good idea,' he nodded. 'We'll see you later, then.'

She looked down at the minute brown bikini she wore. 'Will we need this tomorrow?'

'No.' He packed his equipment away for the day.

'Then I'll wear it back to the hotel.' She pulled on a
wrap, glad to be hidden at last from curious eyes. She
was tall, with the slender figure of a model, her features
classically beautiful, her brown eyes almond-shaped,
slightly tilted at the corners to hint at the Oriental. And
then there was her hair, her beautiful, red-gold hair, the
colour of which could never be matched by anything
out of a bottle. Her features and colouring were instantly
riveting, making her one of the top models in England,
although she doubted she had the ambition to actually
reach the top. As long as she had enough money to
support herself and Tony in comfort then she was
happy.

Dear Tony! If she went back to the hotel now she
might just be in time to call Simon and talk to Tony
before Janice bathed him and put him to bed. Just to
hear his childish lisping of the word 'Mum' would be
enough to make her day.

'Hey, sleepyhead,' Paul interrupted her thoughts. 'I
was talking to you!'

'I'm sorry,' Velvet blinked, her lashes dark and silky.
'What did you say?'

'I said wear the bikini you have on, no one is going to
ask for it back.'

'Wear this!' Velvet scorned. 'You must be joking! It
would probably fall apart in the water.'

He smiled. 'A great advert you are for Style
Swimwear!'

Carly bounced out of the back of the trailer they were
using to change in, dressed in her own tight-fitting
denims and a tee-shirt. 'Ready?' she smiled up at her
boy-friend, her dark attractive features beautiful even
without make-up.

Paul frowned. 'Ready for what?'

'To take me to Ocean World. And don't say you
forgot,' she added as he began to shake his head. 'You

promised, Paul,' she pouted petulantly.

'I have to get this film developed.'

'Ocean World won't take long to see, and it's only just down the road.'

'We're here to work, Carly. I——'

'Oh, don't be such an old grouch, Paul,' Velvet cut in. 'Take Carly to Ocean World.'

'And what do I do if our client asks to see the initial photographs this evening?'

'He's invited us to dinner,' Carly dismissed. 'He'll hardly expect to see the work already completed.'

'I'd forgotten all about dinner this evening,' Velvet frowned. 'Isn't it a little unusual to be invited out by the owner of a firm as big as Style Clothes?'

Paul shrugged. 'It happens. Besides, we're staying at his hotel. He lives in the penthouse apartment.'

She raised her eyebrows. 'I didn't know that.'

'Where did you think we were having dinner?' he teased.

'Not at his apartment.'

'He flew in yesterday evening,' Paul explained. 'I spoke to him last night while the two of you slept.'

Carly wrinkled her nose at him. 'We don't all have your stamina for work. Besides, Velvet and I need our beauty sleep.'

He grinned. 'You said it!'

'Why, you——'

Velvet laughed at Carly's fury. 'I think you walked into that one,' she teased the other girl.

'Maybe,' she admitted grudgingly. 'But just for that,' she put her arm through the crook of Paul's, 'you can definitely take me to Ocean World.'

He sighed. 'Who wants to see a load of dolphins performing tricks?'

'I do,' Carly said firmly. 'And if you aren't careful I'll push you in with the sharks!'

Velvet knew that this veiled argument hid a very real affection, Carly and Paul were very much in love with each other.

'Okay,' Paul gave in. 'Coming with us, Velvet?'

She shook her head. 'I'm going back to the hotel to make a telephone call and then I'm going swimming.'

'Don't be late for dinner,' he warned. 'Seven-thirty for eight in the penthouse suite.'

'I'll be there,' she promised.

'And look your most stunning, I think Daniels will appreciate that.'

She grinned at Paul's determination to impress their employer. 'I'll wear the sexiest dress I can find.'

'Not that one,' he said hastily, obviously recalling the daring of the black gown she had in mind. 'I don't want him to take you to bed, just to realise how beautiful the models are I've brought with me.'

'I'll remember,' and she laughingly took her leave of them. If she didn't soon make that telephone call it would be too late.

Her casual attire was perfectly acceptable in the hotel reception, some of the other people walking about in even less than she was, their nakedness barely covered by swimming attire. Although a model, and reasonably sure of herself, she would have felt too embarrassed to walk in wearing just the bikini she had modelled earlier; it was two strips of material that only just contained her modesty. The matching wrap at least reached down to her thighs, although the material was diaphanous.

But she didn't give the impression of being in the least selfconscious as she strolled across the reception area to the elevator, a tall beautiful girl with strawberry-blonde hair and flashing dark eyes.

'Velvet! Velvet, stop!'

She frowned, turning to face the owner of that deep, attractive voice, a voice as English as her own. A tall man, well over six feet, was making his way towards her, a ruggedly handsome man with dark almost black hair, distinguished wings of grey at his temples, his eyes deeply blue, surrounded by thick black lashes, his nose long and straight, a dark shadow above his top lip over the firmness of his jaw, a shadow that meant he probably had to shave twice a day. Above that strong jawline his top lip jutted out determinedly, the lower lip fuller, hinting at a deep sensuality. He had wide powerful shoulders, tapering to a narrow waist and lean hips, and he was probably the most handsome man Velvet had ever seen. The white trousers fitted to his muscular thighs, the dark blue shirt was partly unbuttoned down his chest, his skin was deeply tanned, as if he lived a lot of his life out in the sun.

Yes, he was very handsome, excitingly so, being in his late thirties or early forties, she would say, having an assurance and confidence about him that pointed to him being unnerved by little. He was also acting as if he knew her, and much as she would like it to be true, she knew she had never seen him in her life before. He just wasn't the sort of man you forgot once you had met him.

'Velvet!' He grasped both her hands in his, searching her face with those deep blue eyes as if he intended memorising every feature. 'My God,' he choked, very pale beneath his tan, a haggard look to his face. 'It really is you!' His hands tightened on hers.

She gave a polite meaningless smile, trying to extricate her hands without causing a scene. Men had tried to pick her up in this way in the past, but never anyone like this man. 'It really is me,' she agreed lightly. 'Now would you mind . . .?' she looked pointedly at their joined hands.

'God, Velvet,' he groaned, making no effort to release her, 'you don't know what it does to me to see you here!'

She was beginning to, his hold on her hands was painful now. 'Could you please let me go?' she winced.

His hold relaxed a little, but he didn't release her. 'Velvet . . .'

She was becoming angry now, aware that they were attracting more than their fair share of attention. 'I think we've established that that is my name,' she said in her coldest voice, realising this man was going to be a difficult one to shake off.

It happened, of course, men claiming they knew her. In her profession it was bound to; men saw her photograph in a magazine and thought it entitled them to claim an acquaintance with her.

Not that this man didn't look as if he would be interesting to know, he did. But she was here to work, and the sooner the work was finished the sooner she would be able to get back to Tony. Tony! Goodness, if she didn't soon make that call Simon and Janice would have gone to bed too!

'It's been pleasant meeting you, Mr—er—— But I have to go now,' she finally managed to release her hand. 'If you'll excuse me . . .' and she turned to leave, already dismissing him from her mind.

A strong hand came out to stop her, blue eyes narrowing as the man moved to stand in front of her. 'Velvet, I know things ended abruptly between us, but I thought you understood——'

'Now look, Mr——'

'Jerard,' he put in tersely.

'Mr Jerard,' she said impatiently. 'You——'

'Just Jerard,' he snapped. 'Don't play games, Velvet, not now, and not with me.'

She pulled out of his grasp, knowing there would be bruises on her wrist tomorrow. Paul would love that! 'I don't play games, Mr—Jerard,' she snapped. 'And I don't particularly like the people who do.'

'I don't play games either,' he rasped. 'I never have.'

'Then I wish you wouldn't now,' she rubbed her tender skin. 'I'm in a hurry, and I really don't have the time to talk to you right now.'

'Velvet!'

She glared up at him. 'Will you please leave me alone!'

He frowned. 'Why are you pretending you don't know me?'

'Because I don't!' she cried her exasperation. 'And if this is a pick-up it really isn't a very original one,' she dismissed scathingly.

'Pick-up!' he exploded, his eyes blazing, a pulse beating irratically at his jaw. 'Don't do this to me, Velvet. I may deserve it, but don't do it.' His expression was haunted.

She shook her head. 'I have no idea what you're talking about.'

'I'm talking about us,' he sighed. 'You and me.'

'There is no you and me. Now if we're supposed to have met in the past, then I'm sorry, but I don't remember the meeting.'

'You do remember,' he snarled, very tense. 'You're just trying to punish me.'

She bit her lip at the savagery of his expression. 'I have no idea what you're talking about. But you and I have never met before. Now I really do have to go.' She brushed past him, and this time he made no effort to stop her.

She was shaking as she stepped into the lift, turning to press the button for her floor, seeing the man called Jerard still standing where she had left him, looking as if she had struck him a physical blow.

What had seemed to be a conventional pick-up, a 'haven't we met before' approach, had turned out to be

something else entirely. The man had to be insane, or
else genuinely suffering from mistaken identity. And yet
he hadn't seemed mistaken, he had even called her by
her name. But she didn't know him, would never forget
such an intense personality. Unless . . .? No, no, it wasn't
possible she had ever met him before.

She put the call through to Simon once she reached
her room, just managing to talk to Tony before Janice
put him to bed. His lisped question of when she was
coming home brought a lump to her throat, and she
quickly reassured him that it would be soon. She had
only left him twice before, and each time it had only
been for two days. Talking to her son like this, made her
conscious of the miles separating them, made her wish
that she had never come to Fort Lauderdale.

'How are you, love?' her brother asked once Tony
had gone off quite happily with his aunt.

'I'm fine,' she told him huskily. 'Is Tony behaving
himself?'

'Does he ever?' Simon laughed.

'Oh dear,' she sighed worriedly. 'What's he done?'

'Nothing too serious. He tried to eat the cat's
food——'

'Ugh!' she grimaced.

'Quite,' he agreed dryly. 'The only thing was he tried
to eat it at the same time as the cat did. You can imagine
what happened!'

'I'm trying not to.' Simon and Janice had a huge grey
tabby, a placid creature, until it came to her food, that
she would defend with her life. 'What happened?'

'Tiger turned round and swiped him one. That's when
Tony grabbed her tail and wouldn't let go.'

Velvet was laughing so much she had tears streaming
down her face—or could they be due to the fact that she
was missing her son so much? 'Who won in the end?'

'I think they called it a draw. Tony had a scratched

hand, and Tiger slunk off into a corner to wash her tail. They're friends again now, though, they've been playing together for the last hour. Now, how's the work going?'

'Quite well. But it's so hot. You know me, I can't stand the heat. Also—No,' Velvet bit her lip, reluctant to tell her brother about the strange man she had just met. 'It doesn't matter,' she dismissed.

'What is it, Velvet?' he asked sharply, always having been the one she ran to with her problems.

'There was this man——'

'Looking the way you do there was bound to be,' he derided.

'No, it wasn't like that, Simon. He—he was so strange.' She went on to describe her meeting with the man called Jerard.

'Did he upset you?' her brother wanted to know.

'Not really,' she frowned. 'He disturbed me more than anything.'

'Good-looking, was he?' Simon teased.

'I didn't mean that sort of disturbed,' she told him crossly, in a way glad that he hadn't taken the incident seriously; it made her feel she didn't have to either.

'I don't see why not—it's some time since Anthony died. You're too young and beautiful to be alone for ever,' he said gently. 'Besides, Tony needs a father.'

'Simon!' she spluttered her indignation. 'This man definitely wasn't father material, not at all,' she added with certainty. 'And even if he were I'm not interested. He was weird,' she shivered, the memory of his fierce blue eyes burning into hers still very much with her.

'Then you make sure you stay away from him,' her brother warned. 'I'd better let you go now, this call must be costing a fortune.'

'Okay. Give Tony a hug for me, and a hug and a kiss for you and Janice.'

'See you soon, love.'

She felt quite dejected once she had rung off, feeling a need to get out of her room and be among people. But she didn't feel like walking back over to the beach, opting to use the hotel pool instead. She just hoped she wouldn't run into that hateful man again!

It seemed her luck was in; there was no sign of the man, and the pool was mainly deserted in favour of the beach. The pool was gloriously cool, and she swam for half an hour or more before getting out to lie on one of the loungers scattered about its edge.

'You swim well,' remarked someone at her side.

Her eyes flickered open to meet warm blue ones; a tall blond American was standing beside her, his tan a golden bronze. But Velvet didn't welcome a pick-up twice in one day. 'Thank you,' she said uninterestedly, closing her eyes again.

'You're one of the models staying here, aren't you?'

Another persistent one! She opened her eyes to find he had sat down on the lounger next to hers. Velvet sat up, the anger in her clear brown eyes shielded by the huge round sun-glasses she wore. 'How did you know that?' she wanted to know.

'I'm the assistant manager here,' he grinned at her, very handsome in a golden sort of way, rather like one of the Greek gods the romantics were always talking about.

Her mouth twitched into an unwilling smile, finally smiling openly. 'That's cheating!'

'I know,' he smiled. 'One of the perks of the job.'

'Chatting up girls?' she teased, knowing this man was someone she could handle.

'You're my first model.' His gaze was appreciative of her slender beauty.

'I'm flattered!' she laughed at his directness. She liked his candidness, although he was nowhere near as excitingly attractive as the man called Jerard.

Just to think of the other man gave her a shiver down her spine—and it wasn't one of fear. That surprised her, she hadn't thought herself that attracted to him. He was the first man she had found remotely interesting since Anthony had died, and she felt a certain amount of resentment towards him for kindling that interest.

'I hope that scowl isn't for me,' the man at her side interrupted her disturbing thoughts.

'I—No,' she gave him a dazzling smile. 'I was thinking of something else.'

'That isn't allowed when you're with me. I'm Greg Boyd, by the way.'

'And I'm Velvet Dale.'

'Oh, I know that,' he grinned. 'I always know the names of the beautiful women staying at the hotel.'

'That must be difficult,' she teased. 'They all look beautiful.'

Greg shook his head. 'Pretty, not beautiful. There's a difference. *You're* beautiful.'

'Thank you,' she accepted the compliment for what it was.

'Care to join me in a drink?' he invited.

'I——' She gave a brief glance at her wrist-watch. It was already five-thirty, time she went back to her room to prepare for the evening ahead. 'No, thanks. I have to go now.'

He watched as she stood up and pulled on her wrap. 'Was it something I said?' He looked crestfallen.

'No,' Velvet laughed at his woebegone expression. 'I just have an appointment this evening, and I think I should go and get ready.'

'Just my luck,' Greg grimaced. 'It's my evening off,' he explained. 'And I'd been hoping you might join me for dinner.'

'Maybe another night.' She picked up her towel and sun-tan oil.

'I don't have another night off this week.'

She gave a lightly teasing smile. 'Then might I suggest another girl?'

He burst out laughing, and stood up too. 'You're a little unusual, aren't you?' He fell into step beside her as they entered the hotel.

'Am I?' she quirked an eyebrow at him.

'You sure are. I like you, Velvet Dale.'

'Mrs Velvet Dale,' she said pointedly.

Greg frowned. 'You're married?'

'Widowed.'

'At your age?'

She shrugged. 'It happens. Besides, twenty-two isn't young any more.'

He pulled a face. 'What does that make me at thirty?'

'Ancient!' She laughed, the laugh dying in her throat as she became aware of piercing blue eyes watching her.

The man called Jerard was walking in the direction of the lift, his fierce gaze fixed savagely on her as she talked to Greg. And he looked furious, so much so that Velvet stayed talking to Greg while the other man got into the lift. She daren't get in there with him, there was no telling what he would do if she did.

It took ages for the lift to come back down again, but luckily it was now empty. She hoped that man's room wouldn't be anywhere near hers.

She hadn't really brought many evening dresses with her, not realising she would be dining with their important client. She wouldn't wear anything too daring, at his age she might give him a heart attack. Charles Daniels must be at least seventy by now. No wonder Paul had warned against the black gown—it really was too seductively daring.

The brown one was ideal, attractive without being too revealing. Her hair was newly washed and gleaming, her make-up light and unobtrusive. She looked beautiful enough to make an impression but not to raise the poor man's blood pressure.

'Perfect,' Paul told her when they called for her.

He was looking very distinguished himself in a black evening suit and white shirt, Carly as beautiful as usual in a clinging black gown.

'How was Ocean World?' Velvet asked them in the lift on the way up to the penthouse suite.

'Well?' Carly looked at Paul for the answer.

'It was—it was good, very good,' he admitted grudgingly. 'Okay, okay,' he sighed at Carly's triumphant look, 'so I enjoyed myself.'

'You'll have to go, Velvet,' the other girl said enthusiastically. 'If Grouchy here liked it then you know it was good.'

Velvet nodded. 'I'll see if I can get there some time tomorrow. I wanted to call my brother this afternoon.'

They stepped out of the lift. 'How's Tony?' Paul enquired.

'Wrecking the place, as usual,' she laughed, looking around her appreciatively. 'This is something, hmm?'

Paul nodded, their surroundings luxurious in the extreme. 'Wait until you meet our host, he's more than just something.'

Velvet laughed. 'Seventy-year-old men don't really appeal to me.' Paul frowned. 'Seventy-year-old——? He isn't seventy, Velvet.'

'But Charles Daniels——'

'Died two years ago. His son's been in charge ever since.'

She blinked. 'His son?'

'Yes, Velvet,' a man appeared from a room to the left of them, a man with startlingly familiar fierce blue eyes. 'I took over from my father,' he confirmed his identity as Charles Daniels' son.

She went pale. This man was the man who had

stopped her in reception earlier, the man who claimed to know her—he was Jerard *Daniels*! Paul was right, he was more than just something, he was overpowering in the white dinner jacket and black trousers, every inch the powerful businessman he undoubtedly was.

He came forward to take her hand, the intensity of his gaze not allowing for the other couple in the room. 'We meet again, Velvet,' he said huskily.

She was mesmerised, held immobile by the intimacy of his expression. 'I—Yes,' she confirmed stupidly.

'The two of you have met before?' Paul sounded puzzled.

'I——'

'A couple of years ago,' Jerard Daniels answered for her. 'Although Velvet chooses not to remember that,' he added harshly.

'I don't choose to, Mr Daniels,' she snapped. 'It happens to be the truth.'

'But I remember you—vividly.'

She blushed at the familiarity in his eyes, her smile strained. 'I'm sorry,' she shook her head, 'but I really have no recollection . . .'

'Never mind,' he put her hand in the crook of his arm, smiling at the other couple. 'Shall we go through and have a drink before dinner?'

For the next fifteen minutes he was everything the polite host should be, although he didn't let Velvet leave his side, his hand snaking out to grasp her wrist if she should attempt to do so.

He frightened her. There was about him an air of suppressed violence, a dangerous quality to him that disturbed her.

'Have you lived in Florida long, Mr Daniels?' Carly asked him as they ate their dinner, Velvet placed opposite him at the long table.

'Jerard,' he put in smoothly. 'And I don't live here,

Carly. I'm only here at all because Velvet is.'

'Oh.' Carly sounded unsure of his direct answer.

Colour blazed in Velvet's cheeks at the puzzled glances Paul and Carly kept shooting her. This man was embarrassing her, was giving her friends the impression that they had a relationship. 'Is your wife with you, Mr Daniels?' she asked waspishly.

His expression darkened, his gaze rapier-sharp as he looked at her. 'My wife is dead, Velvet,' he rasped.

'Oh!' She moved uncomfortably. 'I—I'm sorry.'

'She isn't,' he said abruptly. 'To die from heart disease isn't very pleasant.'

'Oh.'

His eyes narrowed. 'And your husband is dead too.'

She blinked at him, bewildered by his knowledge of her when she knew absolutely nothing about him. 'He died in a flying accident,' she supplied.

'I know that too—you were a passenger. You were carrying his child at the time.'

She swallowed hard. 'I—Yes.'

In that moment Jerard Daniels looked satanic, as if he would like to hit out and hurt someone. He seemed to control this urge with effort. 'You have a son,' he said in a curious flat voice.

'Tony, yes.'

'Named after his father.'

'I—yes. You see, Anthony never saw him. He was born on the day Anthony died.' She didn't know why she was explaining herself to this man, her life with Anthony had nothing whatsoever to do with him.

'I have a daughter,' Jerard Daniels told her.

'You do?' she asked interestedly, her assumption that this man wasn't father material instantly contradicted.

He was watching her closely. 'She's eight years old.'

'Is she here with you?' Carly wanted to know, obviously feeling that she and Paul had been excluded from the conversation long enough.

Jerard Daniels smiled at her, a completely charming smile. 'Not at the moment, no. She'll be joining me soon.'

'That will be nice for you,' Carly responded to that smile, instantly captivated.

'Very nice,' he nodded. 'How's the photography going, Paul?' He suddenly seemed to be remembering his manners.

Velvet relaxed for the first time since she had entered the apartment and discovered Jerard Daniels was their host, his attention at last removed from her. How did he know all those things about her life? And why did he maintain that they had met before when she knew they hadn't?

She listened to his conversation, sensing that he knew almost as much about photography as Paul did. He was a man who would have a knowledge of many things— and she seemed to be one of them!

Carly was giving her a frowning look, as if to say 'What's with you two?' She wished she knew that herself? She shrugged at the other girl, knowing that Carly was curious about the past relationship Jerard kept insisting they had had. Well, she was curious about it herself!

She wanted to excuse herself after dinner was over, but the two men were still discussing photography, making it highly unlikely that Paul would want to leave just yet. And she could hardly leave without him and Carly, not without making a scene.

So she sat in one of the armchairs, a polite smile of interest fixed falsely on her face as she tried desperately to remember if she and Jerard Daniels *had* ever met before. He was so adamant that they had, and he didn't seem the type to lie about something like that. Besides, he was very attractive, having charmed Carly until she was starry-eyed, so he didn't need to go to such extremes to get a woman.

She watched him as he talked to Paul. He really was very attractive, in a harsh sort of way. Still, it sounded as if life had dealt him a series of hard blows lately, first of all his wife dying of heart disease and then his father dying too. But she really couldn't say she knew him.

Maybe she reminded him of his wife or something? She could come up with any number of excuses for his mistake in thinking he knew her, but she had no way of knowing if any of them were right.

When Paul finally suggested they leave she stood hurriedly to her feet, eager to be gone.

Once again Jerard Daniels took hold of her arm, holding her easily at his side. 'You two go ahead,' he said politely to Paul and Carly. 'I just want to have a private word with Velvet.'

She swallowed hard. 'It's late, Mr Daniels,' she told him sharply. 'Perhaps we can talk in the morning?'

'Tonight,' he insisted in a hard voice that brooked no argument. 'Now.'

'I——'

'We'll see you in the morning, Velvet,' said Paul before he and Carly stepped into the lift.

'How dare you!' Velvet turned angrily on Jerard Daniels once they were alone, forgetting for the moment that he was employing her, remembering only that he had embarrassed her. 'You know what they're thinking!'

He raised one dark eyebrow. 'And what would that be?'

'That I'm spending the night up here with you!' she snapped, two bright spots of angry colour in her cheeks.

He looked unconcerned. 'So?'

'So I want to leave now. Look, I'm sorry if I don't

remember meeting you before, but I meet such a lot of people in my profession. If we were friends——'

'We were a little more than that, Velvet,' he revealed tightly, his features set in harsh lines.

She looked at him dazedly, licking her lips nervously. 'You mean . . .?'

He gave an arrogant inclination of his head. 'I mean we were lovers, Velvet.'

CHAPTER TWO

SHE pulled out of his grasp. 'I don't believe you!' she gasped.

His eyes were narrowed to icy slits. 'It's the truth, I can assure you. I loved you, I thought you loved me too. It seems I was just the first man in your life,' he rasped.

Her eyes were wide with shock. 'The first . . .'

'I was your first lover, Velvet. You were a virgin when we made love.' His mouth twisted bitterly.

'I—I—Oh God!' She turned away, shaking with reaction. 'This can't be happening to me,' she groaned.

Jerard walked past her into the lounge, poured out two brandies and handed her one. 'Drink it,' he ordered, swallowing his own in one gulp, unmoved by the fiery liquid.

Velvet took a tentative sip, grimacing at the unaccustomed alcohol. She never drank alcohol, had always had an aversion to it.

'I think you'd better go,' Jerard Daniels said harshly. 'We obviously have nothing to talk about.'

'I—No. I—Yes, I—I'll go,' and she turned blindly in the direction of the lift.

'But first——' he swung her round to face him, 'first I get to kiss the woman who's haunted my days and invaded my nights for longer than I care to remember!' His mouth ground down on hers, demanding that she respond.

No man had kissed her since Anthony, no one had been allowed close enough to take this liberty. But

27

Jerard Daniels wasn't going to ask her permission; he took what he wanted, uncaring whether or not she enjoyed it.

But she was enjoying it, had melted at the first pressure of his lips on hers, gave herself up to the pleasure he was evoking—was even managing to kiss him back.

Suddenly his mouth gentled on hers, tasting her lips like a thirsty man in the desert craves water. His hands moved caressingly across her bare back, probing the line of her shoulder-blade and shooting spasms of pleasure through her body.

Velvet groaned with the familiarity of his movements, distant memories flashing into her brain, memories that faded before she could recall the reality of them.

This man *had* kissed her before, had touched her, she knew it as surely as she breathed. She just didn't remember it!

He swung her up into his arms, still kissing her as he carried her into one of the bedrooms, kicking the door shut behind them.

The slam of the door was enough to bring her to her senses, and she started to struggle as he gently laid her down on the bed, clearly intending to join her. 'No!' She broke away from him.

'No?' he groaned in raw agony, his eyes glazed with passion.

'No,' she choked, scrambling off the bed. 'I—I don't know what happened just now——'

'You wanted me,' he rasped. 'That's what happened.'

Velvet blushed at the accuracy of his words. She had wanted him, and that had never happened to her before with a complete stranger. But was he a stranger? He didn't seem to think so—and neither did her body.

'And I wanted you,' he added sneeringly. 'How does it make you feel to know that after all this time I still want you? Does it give you a cheap thrill to know that I was completely taken in by you and the love you professed to have for me?'

Velvet swallowed hard, frightened of his anger. 'I——' she licked her lips. 'I——'

'You're speechless, hmm?' he derided bitterly. 'I thought we had something special, Velvet, the sort of love that would last even though we were apart.'

She frowned. 'I'm sorry . . .'

Jerard Daniels' eyes flashed deeply blue. 'Get out of here!' he snapped. 'I've been in love with a dream all this time. But I can see the reality now, can see that I meant nothing to you. How could I?' he scorned. 'You didn't waste any time getting married, did you, and to your nice respectable lawyer.'

'Anthony . . .?'

'Yes, Anthony Dale!' he rasped. 'How long did you wait, Velvet? One week, two? It couldn't have been much more than that!'

She shook her head. 'I don't——'

'You don't remember!' he cut in furiously. 'No, I realise you don't. I was just one of the men stupid enough to fall in love with you. I thought I meant something to you, that we had something special, but we obviously didn't.'

'Please,' she begged. 'You don't understand——'

'But I do—finally,' he said heavily. 'Goodbye, Velvet.'

'Please, let me——'

'Go!' He scowled at her, walking out to the lounge and picking up the whisky bottle and a glass before returning to the bedroom. He threw himself down on the bed, pouring some of the whisky into a glass. 'Close the door on your way out.' He threw the whisky to the back of his throat before refilling the glass to the rim.

Velvet stumbled from the room, almost running to the lift. That Jerard Daniels intended getting drunk she had no doubt. She only wished she could drown her own pain in the same way.

But alcohol wasn't the answer for her, she needed a clear head to work out this puzzle. But it wasn't such a puzzle, it was more of a blank, a blank that she would possibly never fill.

She had wanted to explain to Jerard Daniels, to tell him *why* she didn't remember him, but she had a feeling that the truth would be even harder for him to understand and believe.

She reached her room without seeing anyone, knowing that if she had they might wonder what had so upset her that she was as white as a sheet.

The doctors at the hospital had told her that it had been the shock, the shock of losing Anthony and the birth of little Tony. She had woken up in a hospital bed with the last eleven months missing out of her life, knowing only that she had lost the husband that she loved, and that she had given birth to his child.

She and Anthony had been going out together for eighteen months, had been engaged for six months of that time, and she knew that she loved him. But all their married life together was a blank to her, the trauma of his death had erased their marriage from her memory.

And now Jerard Daniels claimed to have met her during that blank eleven months, claimed they had been lovers, that he had been her *first* lover. She knew that she and Anthony hadn't made love before the blank in her life, and had loved Anthony all the more for respecting her wish that they marry first.

Anthony had been older than she, was a friend of her brother's to start with. She had been nineteen when they first met, had liked his blond good looks and serious manner. He had belonged to the same law firm as Simon, but was new to town, so Simon had taken him under his wing and brought him home to dinner. Velvet had been living with Simon at the time, their parents having recently emigrated to Australia to be close to their other son Nigel, and his wife Jennifer. Velvet was supposed to have joined them, but once she had met Anthony she had refused to go, continuing to live with Simon and Janice until she married Anthony.

So where did Jerard Daniels fit into the nice tidy pattern of her life, where did he fit into that blank eleven months? Only he could tell her the answer to that question, and after the way they had parted this evening she doubted he would be in any mood to tell her anything.

This had never happened before. No one else had come forward and claimed to have met her during that time. In fact she had come to accept the blank, to accept her life as it now was, certain that her marriage to Anthony had been as successful as the rest of their relationship. Simon had assured her it was—Simon! Perhaps he would know something about Jerard Daniels? Perhaps she would call him tomorrow and find out.

She wasn't able to sleep, disturbed and upset by this strange turn of events. How could she have taken a lover when she was engaged to Anthony? How could she have taken a lover at all! She didn't believe it, couldn't believe it. Especially a man like Jerard Daniels! Anthony had been ten years her senior, but Jerard Daniels must be even older than that, and she just couldn't believe she was ever involved with such a man. If only he weren't so adamant!

She had been up and dressed for hours when Carly knocked on her door, and had been expecting the barrage of questions that came her way from the other girl.

'What time did you leave Jerard's apartment last night?' Carly asked eagerly.

'Just after you,' Velvet answered rigidly.

'Really?' Carly looked disappointed.

'Yes, really,' she sighed.

'What did he want to talk to you about, then?'

'Just work,' she shrugged.

Carly gave her a scornful glance. 'I'll bet!'

'Carly——'

'Look, Velvet,' Carly grinned, 'it was obvious the man fancies you like hell.'

'He——'

'He wants to sleep with you,' Carly insisted.

'Maybe,' Velvet admitted grudgingly, knowing that last night that had been true.

'No maybe about it,' Carly scoffed. 'Paul and I could feel the air sizzle every time he looked at you. It was a relief to get away from the heat!' she grinned.

Velvet blushed. 'I—He——'

'He asked for you especially, you know.'

She gave the other girl a startled glance. 'What do you mean?'

Carly sat down on the bed, and Velvet faced her across the room from the chair in front of the dressing-table. She shrugged. 'Paul thought he'd asked for you because he'd seen some of your other work and liked the look of you. But after last night, after finding that you two had met before, we realised that had been the reason he requested you on this job.'

Velvet frowned. 'You're saying that Jerard Daniels asked Paul to bring me here?'

'Exactly,' Carly nodded.

Velvet didn't like that, just as she didn't like the fact that Jerard Daniels seemed to know so much about her life. It was like an invasion of privacy, leaving her naked and defenceless.

She stood up briskly. 'Are we working today?'

Carly looked disappointed. 'Does that mean the subject of Jerard Daniels is closed?'

'Very much so,' Velvet nodded.

'Will it always be?'

'I'm not sure, but I think so.'

'Shame,' Carly sighed. 'You meet some creeps in this line of work, but he's such an interesting individual. Interesting!' she dismissed in disgust. 'He's gorgeous. Tall, dark, and mysterious.'

Velvet smiled. 'And Paul?'

'Oh, heavens—Paul! We're supposed to be meeting him in reception. He wants us all to have an early breakfast and then get to work before it gets too hot.'

'Good idea. The heat finished me off yesterday.'

'Me too,' Carly grimaced. 'And if we don't go down now Paul will probably complete the job.'

Velvet laughed. 'Then let's go.'

Paul was scowling when they stepped out of the lift. 'I thought I told you not to stop and ask questions,' he told Carly impatiently, marching them both into the dining-room.

Carly poked her tongue out at him across the table. 'Only because you wanted to know the answers yourself. And they say women are nosey!'

He gave the waitress three orders of coffee and toast, scowling heavily at his girl-friend. 'Velvet's relationship with Mr Daniels is none of our business,' he hissed.

'Who says so?' she scorned.

'He does,' Paul sighed.

Velvet frowned. 'When did he tell you that?'

'Just now, on his way to the airport.'

He had gone; Jerard Daniels had left! Velvet felt the tension draining out of her. 'He had no need to do that,' she said lightly, feeling suddenly free now that she knew he wasn't going to suddenly appear. 'We really didn't have a relationship.' Not one she remembered anyway. 'And I didn't want toast for my breakfast, Paul,' she effectively changed the subject, 'just coffee.'

'You'll eat the toast,' he growled. 'You hardly ate any dinner last night.'

She smiled. 'I won't kid myself that you're concerned for my health.'

His mouth twitched and then he too smiled. 'Sorry, Velvet. I think the heat is getting to me too.'

'I should treasure that apology, Velvet,' Carly put in cheekily. 'It's almost unheard-of.'

Both girls burst out laughing at Paul's outraged expression, and soon he joined in.

The subject of Jerard Daniels seemed to be forgotten by the other couple, so Velvet decided to do the same. She wouldn't bother to call Simon about the other man, not now that he had left the hotel. If it was still bothering her when she got home she could ask her brother about it then.

Greg Boyd had just come into the dining-room, dressed much more formally than yesterday as he came over to their table, his grey lightweight suit and white shirt very smart, as was the rest of his neatly groomed appearance.

'Hi,' he greeted them with a smile.

'Good morning,' Velvet returned with a smile, and made the introductions.

He sat down at the fourth chair at their table. 'I'm going to be free this afternoon,' he told Velvet. 'I wondered if you would be too.'

'You'll have to ask Paul that.'

He looked at the other man. 'Well?'

'Why not?' Paul shrugged. 'It's too hot to work in the afternoons anyway.'

'So gracious!' Carly grimaced.

Paul quirked an eyebrow at her. 'I thought you wanted me to drive you to the Everglades?'

'I do,' she nodded eagerly.

'Then shut up.'

Velvet laughed. 'Don't mind them, Greg,' she advised at his worried frown. 'They love each other really.'

'Huh!' Paul scoffed.

'I have vays of making you suffer,' Carly said in her most ham German accent.

'Sexual threats, no less,' Paul taunted.

'Are you sure they love each other?' Greg teased.

'Very sure,' Velvet laughed. 'They just have a strange way of showing it.'

'You're not kidding,' he drawled.

Paul put his arm about Carly's shoulders. 'I might even make an honest woman out of her one day.'

'You should be so lucky,' she answered in a disgruntled voice.

He nuzzled his lips against her earlobe. 'I will be.'

'Huh!' but Carly was obviously weakening towards him, and snuggled into his arms for further kisses.

'It's enough to put you off your breakfast,' Velvet teased.

'It sure is,' Greg grinned. 'So about this afternoon . . .'

'Come with us, if you like,' Paul invited.

'I'd like to, but I don't really have the time to go that far. I have to be back on duty at six,' Greg explained regretfully.

'How far are the Everglades?' Paul groaned.

'About an hour's journey either way, and then there's the two-hour trip round. You won't see anything if you don't take the tour.'

'Oh God,' Paul moaned. 'I hate organised tours.'

'Then cycle round,' Greg suggested. 'It's only fifteen miles, and you can hire a cycle there.'

'Cycle!' Carly burst out laughing at Paul's stunned expression. 'When did you last ride a bicycle, darling?' she mocked.

'When did you?' he scowled.

'About six months ago, for an advert I was working on.'

'As I recall you *sat* on it, you didn't ride it,' he

scorned. 'I think we'll skip the bicycle ride,' he told Greg, 'and take the tour after all.'

Greg nodded. 'It's worth it. I guarantee you'll enjoy it. But don't expect the Everglades to be like the Hollywood producers would have you believe in the films they make about it. It's basically flat, no tall trees, with occasional small tree islands.'

'Oh.' Carly sounded disappointed.

'Parts of it are like they show in the movies,' Greg consoled her. 'I'm just warning you that the majority of it isn't.'

'Still want to go?' Paul asked her.

'I'm not sure . . .'

'I didn't mean to put you off,' Greg sighed.

'You haven't,' Carly gave him a bright smile. 'We'll go,' she told Paul. 'Maybe I'll feed you to an alligator.'

'Sharks, and now alligators! I'm beginning to think you don't love me any more,' he mocked.

She gave him a sweet saccharine smile. 'Maybe I don't.'

'Liar!' he laughed.

Greg grinned, 'You two are really something!'

'Aren't they?' Velvet laughed.

'Where shall we go this afternoon?' Greg asked her.

'How about Ocean World?'

He grinned. 'Why is it that all the girls I date want to go to Ocean World?'

She couldn't help smiling. 'How many times have you been?'

'About fifty—this year!'

Paul spluttered with laughter. 'You poor devil! Was it worth it?'

The other man smiled. 'Most times, yes.'

'I think they're getting personal,' Carly told Velvet in a stage whisper.

Velvet knew they were. She liked Greg very much,

but she had no intention of sleeping with him. 'Are we going to get any work done today?' she asked in a stilted voice.

Paul pushed away his empty coffee cup. 'I'm ready.'

'And me.' Carly gulped down the last of her coffee, then stood up. 'See you outside, Velvet,' and she pulled Paul away.

'That remark wasn't meant for you, Velvet,' Greg told her anxiously, having noticed her withdrawal, as had the other couple.

'Wasn't it?' she said tautly. 'I don't know what you've heard about models, Greg, but I can assure you that most of us are very hardworking, and have husbands or steady boy-friends.'

'Do you have a steady boy-friend?'

'No. I'm the exception.'

'Well, I may not be a boy, being thirty and ancient, but I would like to be your friend,' he said seriously. 'I like you, Velvet. I just want to spend some time with you.'

She gave him a searching look. 'Is that all?'

'Scout's honour.'

'Were you ever a Boy Scout?'

'No,' he grinned.

Velvet shook her head. 'I thought not. Look, I think I should warn you that you're wasting your time if you want anything more than friendship from me. I have a young son in England that I would like to be able to look straight in the eye when I get home. I don't sleep around.' But she had once slept with Jerard Daniels, according to him. And she had the feeling it was the truth; the sure way he had found the sensitive areas of her body had seemed to indicate previous knowledge of her in particular. She blushed as she remembered the way he had caressed her back, seeming to know exactly the right places to touch.

'I understand that, Velvet,' Greg told her softly. 'And I'm not denying that I wish it could be different. But I knew straight away what sort of girl you are. And I still want to take you to Ocean World.' She laughed. 'For the fifty-first time—this year?'

'It could be the hundredth and I'd still want to take you.'

'Okay,' she stood up. 'What time shall I meet you?'

'Two o'clock in reception?'

'Fine,' she nodded. 'And now I really do have to get to work.'

'So do I.' He held up his hand in a casual wave.

Carly and Paul were waiting outside in the van, Paul obviously not pleased at this further delay, and Carly agog with the existence of Greg.

'I'm beginning to wonder about you, Velvet,' she teased. 'You have men appearing from everywhere!'

'I met Greg yesterday, and——'

'You don't have to explain yourself to us,' Carly cut in. 'You're free, over twenty-one. It's just that I've never seen you with any man before, and two in two days comes as something of a shock.'

'Mr Daniels doesn't count. He——'

'He looked as if he counted to me,' Paul scoffed. 'The man's mad about you.'

Velvet flushed. 'He isn't! He——'

'You really don't have to explain to us, Velvet,' he said gently. 'We're just glad to see you coming alive again. You're too young and beautiful to be alone for ever.'

'Tony needs me,' she defended.

'And what do you need?' Paul quirked an eyebrow at her.

Her blush deepened. 'Not *that*; that's for sure,' she snapped, the memory of her reaction to Jerard Daniels still too vivid for comfort.

Paul's mouth twisted. 'Believe me, Velvet, everyone needs "that". It's just that some people are able to suppress the feelings.'

'Then I must be one of them!'

He shook his head. 'You have to be kidding!'

'Paul——'

'He's only teasing, Velvet——'

'No, I'm not Carly,' he said firmly. 'I think we've known Velvet long enough to be able to talk bluntly.'

'Not that bluntly,' Carly warned.

'Velvet?'

She sighed. 'It isn't that I don't appreciate what you're saying, it's just that at the moment Tony comes first in my life.'

'That doesn't mean there isn't room for a man too.'

'Well, neither Jerard Daniels or Greg fits the bill.'

'Okay,' Paul shruggingly accepted her reluctance to discuss it.

The heat seemed even more unbearable today, so much so that she finally couldn't stand it another moment longer, and ran into the refreshing blue sea. It was beautiful, cool and clean, and she swam for ten minutes or more before rejoining Carly and Paul on the sand, where Paul was just packing his camera equipment away for the day.

His gaze ran over her appreciatively. 'You're right about these costumes, Velvet, they're useless for actually swiming in. It didn't fall apart,' he grinned, 'but it did become transparent!'

Consternation washed over her face and she grabbed a wrap to pull on over the bikini that now showed every curve of her body as if she were naked.

'I should have known!' she said angrily, her embarrassment very acute.

Paul still smiled. 'I'm not complaining.'

Carly punched him on the arm. 'I am. Keep your eyes off!'

'Spoilsport!' he moaned, holding his bruised arm.

'I'm going to get dressed,' and Velvet marched off to the van.

Carly followed her, chuckling at her furious expression. 'It wasn't that bad,' she teased.

'It was awful!' Velvet's face was still bright red. 'Jerard Daniels shouldn't be allowed to sell these!' She threw the bikini down in disgust.

Carly changed too. 'The price he's asking for them I doubt they would normally get wet.'

Velvet didn't know how she was going to face Paul again, never having gone in for any of the semi-nude modelling that some of her friends had.

But she needn't have worried. He had forgotten all about it by the time she and Carly returned to the beach, more concerned with the fact that he got sand in his camera.

'I'll have to clean this out,' he muttered. 'I'm sorry, Carly, but the Everglades are out for this afternoon. Why the hell Daniels insisted we come out here to take the photographs, instead of in a studio like we usually do with beachwear, I just don't know. Florida is all wrong for this type of work. The light is all wrong, the wind is too strong, it's too damned hot, and worst of all, it's playing havoc with my camera equipment.' He scowled heavily.

Velvet had a feeling she knew exactly why Jerard Daniels had wanted them to come out to Florida. He had wanted *her* here, and this had been his way of doing it.

'Would you like to come with Greg and me this afternoon?' she asked Carly.

'No, I'll stay and keep Paul company.'

'Sure?' She was now regretting her decision to accompany Greg, and having Carly with them would take away the impression of a twosome.

'Sure,' Carly nodded.

Greg proved to be an entertaining companion, standing patiently beside her as they watched the keepers getting into the pool to feed the sharks, saw the sea-lion show, and watched the dolphins perform their endearing tricks. Velvet loved the lazy dolphin most of all, because she appeared to do everything wrong but in reality performed some quite amazing antics.

As they came down the steps from the top of the dolphin pool the woman in front of Velvet suddenly seemed to falter, lose her step and fall down the last three stairs to the ground. She let out a cry as she landed awkwardly on her ankle, and the little girl at her side bent down anxiously.

'It's all right, Vicki,' the woman instantly assured her, her pretty face creased up in pain. 'I'm all right.'

Velvet and Greg reached the bottom of the stairs in seconds, going down on their haunches beside the woman, a small pretty brown-haired woman of perhaps thirty, her distressed brown eyes and white face evidence of the pain she was trying to hide from her little girl.

The little girl was perhaps six or seven years in age, dressed in denims and a tee-shirt that showed the thinness of her body, her dark hair long and straight, her eyes a deep, deep blue. She was a pretty child, and she looked more than a little upset by her mother's accident.

'Your ankle?' Greg took charge with the minimum of fuss.

'Yes,' the woman groaned, obviously in agony.

'I'll get you to the hospital,' Greg said grimly.

The little girl seemed to recoil, and moved back against the wall, her eyes wide with fear.

'It's all right, Vicki,' the woman struggled to sit up, her voice distinctly English. 'Vicki!' She held out her hand to the little girl.

'No,' the girl shook her head, 'I won't go to hospital. I won't!'

Velvet instantly went to her side. 'It's all right, darling. No one will hurt you at the hospital,' she soothed.

The girl huddled into her side. 'They kill people there,' she shuddered.

Velvet was taken aback by this statement, and looked frowningly at the injured woman.

'Could you possibly take Vicki back to the hotel?' the woman requested.

'Well, I——'

'That's a good idea, Velvet,' Greg interrupted. 'You take care of Vicki and I'll get this lady to hospital.'

Velvet took one look at the frightened little girl and knew that it was the wisest course of action; Vicki was likely to become hysterical if subjected to a visit to the hospital she so dreaded.

'How about an ice-cream before we go home, Vicki?' she coaxed the little girl.

'I—I'm not sure,' she looked up warily, the lashes surrounding her deep blue eyes ridiculously long. 'Faye?' she looked at the woman for the answer.

'Go with—Velvet?—Go with Velvet, Vicki. Mr Boyd will take me to get my ankle seen to.'

Velvet frowned. Did Greg actually know this couple? And it didn't sound as if the woman and the little girl were mother and daughter after all, maybe they were sisters instead.

'They're staying at the hotel, Velvet,' Greg explained, helping Faye to her feet. 'Take Vicki back there and wait for us.'

'No ice-cream?' Vicki pouted.

'Yes, you can have an ice-cream,' Greg grinned at her, swinging Faye up into his arms. 'But don't be too long getting back to the hotel,' he warned Velvet. 'I doubt we'll be late.' He strode off.

'But I——' He'd gone! She looked down at Vicki, grinning to reassure her. 'Banana split?'

She licked her lips in anticipation. 'Lovely!'

The little girl's fright seemed to be forgotten as she ploughed her way through the huge banana split Velvet ordered for her in the ice-cream parlour they found. Velvet settled for a chocolate milk shake, not the watery type you usually got served in England; the straw stood up in this one, which was so thick she could hardly suck it up the straw.

Vicki sat back once she had finished her ice-cream. 'Could you tell me the time, please?'

Velvet had to stop herself smiling, the little girl's manner was so grown-up. 'It's ten past five.'

'Then we should be getting back.' Vicki got down off her stool, looking up at Velvet expectantly. 'My father will be back now. He'll be getting worried about me.'

Velvet raised her eyebrows, taking Vicki's hand as they went out to get in the taxi she had ordered. 'You're here with your father?'

'Oh yes,' Vicki nodded. 'My mother d-died, and—and Faye takes care of me.'

'I'm sorry, darling,' Velvet squeezed the hand that had trustingly stayed in hers. 'But Faye is nice, isn't she?'

'I don't know. She hasn't been my—my friend very long, just a few months, only since Mummy died really.'

The loss was obviously a recent one, and by Vicki's age she would guess her mother couldn't have been very old. It was also natural to assume that she had died in a hospital, hence the child's aversion to them. It must have been very rough on a little girl of this age, old enough to understand what was happening, but not old enough to understand why.

'Are you going to be my friend?' Vicki asked her shyly.

'Of course I am,' Velvet smiled, as the two of them got out of the taxi as they reached the hotel. 'I can always do with an extra friend, Vicki.' She led the way into the hotel, already feeling a bond developing between them.

Vicki let out a squeal of delight, letting go of Velvet's hand to run over to the man pacing up and down the reception area. 'Daddy!' she cried before launching herself into his arms.

Velvet swallowed hard, keeping to the background. The man now holding Vicki in his arms was none other than Jerard Daniels, which meant that Vicki must be the eight-year-old daughter he had spoken of.

He turned and saw her, his eyes narrowing to icy slits, his face harsh. His long strides brought him quickly to her side. 'Do I take it you're the young woman that stupid idiot entrusted my daughter to?' he rasped.

She gulped. There could be no doubt about his fury, he was absolutely white with it, although his voice was controlled enough, probably for Vicki's sake.

She had thought he had left the hotel, gone back to England. 'You're still here,' she said dazedly.

'Of course I'm still here,' he snapped. 'Where the

hell else would I be?'

'But I—You went to the airport.'

He nodded grimly. 'To collect Vicki, and that idiotic woman who will leave my employment as soon as she's well enough to walk.'

She blinked. 'Faye?'

'Yes.'

'How is she?'

'She has a broken ankle,' his mouth twisted. 'She's lucky she doesn't have a broken neck to go with it!'

Velvet shook her head. 'Sorry?'

'So will she be when she's well enough to listen to what I think of her, just dumping my daughter on a perfect stranger!'

She gasped. 'She didn't dump Vicki on me. She was in pain, her ankle obviously needed expert attention, and Greg——'

'Who the hell is Greg?' he cut in furiously.

'The assistant manager here.'

Jerard Daniels gave a deeply impatient sigh. 'And where does he fit into all this?'

'You mean you don't know?'

'Would I be asking if I did?' he asked with veiled violence, Vicki still held firmly in his arms.

'No, I suppose not.' He had intended making her feel foolish—and he had succeeded. 'Greg and I were at Ocean World when Faye fell. Greg took her to the hospital. I thought he must have called you.'

'No, Miss Rogers did that,' he said grimly. 'Babbling on about leaving Vicki with some woman who just happened to be there.'

'Velvet, Daddy,' Vicki put in. 'She's nice,' she told him conspiratorially.

Velvet felt grateful for the support of one of the Daniels family; she obviously wasn't going to get any support from Jerard Daniels. He was treating her almost like a criminal.

'Faye—Miss Rogers didn't just leave Vicki with a stranger,' she told him coldly. 'Greg recognised her, and she recognised him. She probably thought I worked at the hotel too——'

'Instead of which you're his girl-friend,' he scoffed.

'I'm a friend,' she said firmly.

'She's my friend too, Daddy,' Vicki put in innocently.

'How nice!' he scorned.

'I bet she'd be your friend too, Daddy, if you asked her.'

He looked up at his daughter, his face softening into a smile. 'I already did ask her, poppet,' he said huskily. 'She said no.'

Vicki thought for a moment, frowning. 'Maybe you didn't ask her properly,' she said slowly. 'If you pulled a face at her you probably frightened her.'

'Pulled a face?' he queried softly.

'Yes, you know, like this.' She did a good impression of his furious expression of a few minutes ago. 'Like that, Daddy,' she told him seriously.

Velvet had to once again stop herself from smiling, but the impulse quickly died as Jerard Daniels scowled at her.

'Yes, just like that, Daddy,' Vicki cried excitedly.

It really was too much for Velvet, she couldn't contain her amusement any longer, chuckling softly.

'I'm glad you find it amusing, Mrs Dale,' Jerard Daniels rapped out. 'But I didn't find it in the least amusing as I waited here for the return of my daughter—if she did return. Say goodnight to Mrs Dale, Vicki,' he ordered tautly. 'We have to go now.'

Consternation washed over Velvet. 'Mr Daniels——'

'Say goodnight, Vicki.' He was unrelenting.

''Night, Velvet.' The little girl yawned tiredly, her

head dropping down on to her father's shoulder; her long flight had obviously tired her as much as anything. 'Will I see you tomorrow?'

'I——' Velvet looked at Jerard Daniels' haughty expression. 'You might,' she compromised.

'I hope so,' she murmured, already half asleep.

Her father's expression as he walked off with her in his arms left Velvet in no doubt as to his opinion of her seeing his daughter again tomorrow or any other time.

Long after she reached her room she remembered what Vicki had said about her mother dying recently. If she had died *recently*, then that meant Jerard Daniels had been married at the time he claimed *they* had been lovers!

CHAPTER THREE

She joined Carly and Paul in the dining-room for dinner, having no real appetite for the food, not after the scene she had been through with Jerard Daniels.

'What was going on earlier in reception?' Carly broke into her thoughts. 'I thought Mr Daniels was going to get violent.'

'Carly!' Paul warned, frowning heavily. 'When are you going to learn to mind your own business?'

'Never,' she grinned. 'I'm nosey, I don't mind admitting it.'

Her boy-friend sighed. 'I'm sorry about this, Velvet. She's incorrigible!'

Velvet smiled. 'I don't mind. I just didn't see you at the time.'

'We were in the lounge,' Carly revealed. 'Mr Daniels had been fuming up and down the reception area for an hour before you came in. I've never seen anyone that angry before, I thought he was going to explode. What happened?'

She explained the situation to them—after all, she owed it to them to do so, it could affect their job here.

Carly whistled through her teeth. 'So that was his little girl.'

'Mm,' Velvet nodded. 'She's a sweet little thing, a bit on the small side for eight, but very bright.'

'He seems very fond of her.'

'And no doubt he is,' she busied herself arranging her napkin. 'Vicki certainly idolises him.' That much had been obvious.

'It's a bit rough on a child to lose her mother at that

age,' Paul echoed her own sentiments.

Velvet bit her lip. 'I hope she's going to be all right, now that Faye's hurt.'

'It's Daniels' problem,' Paul dismissed as their meal arrived. 'Let him deal with it.'

Velvet knew that Jerard Daniels wouldn't appreciate her concern, anyway. But she couldn't help worrying. Vicki had so recently lost her mother, and now she had lost what Velvet presumed to be her nanny. Unless Jerard Daniels could be persuaded to forget the incident! After all, what had the poor woman done besides taking the only course of action she could in the circumstances?

But Jerard Daniels wouldn't appreciate her interference. Still, what did she have to lose. Not a lot; Jerard Daniels was already furious with her, why not let him go the whole way and be absolutely livid?

Paul was studying her. 'You look as if you just came to a decision.'

Velvet smiled. 'I did.'

'One you aren't going to let us in on, hmm?'

'Right,' she nodded.

'Sounds interesting,' Carly grinned.

'Sounds private,' Paul corrected. 'You know the meaning of that word, do you?'

'Spoilsport!' she grimaced at him.

Greg joined them as they had their coffee in the lounge, sitting down. 'I can't stay long, I'm on duty. And after the bawling out I got earlier I daren't be caught slacking. Boy, Mr Daniels really laid into me!'

'About his daughter,' Velvet nodded.

'You too, hmm?'

'I'm afraid so,' she said ruefully.

Greg shook his head. 'He was really mad.'

'I know,' she grimaced. 'How's Miss Rogers' ankle now?'

'They're keeping her in for a few days.'

'Poor woman.' Especially as she was probably going to lose her job over it.

'Mm,' Greg nodded. 'They only got here this morning.' He sighed. 'I suppose I should have called Mr Daniels this afternoon, but Faye insisted on doing it herself. I don't think she could have made much sense, not by his reaction to me tonight. You would have thought I'd pushed the woman,' he added with disgust.

'At least he didn't think you'd tried to kidnap his daughter,' Velvet said dryly.

'From that remark I take it he thought you had. I don't understand Mr Daniels this trip,' Greg frowned. 'He's usually such a nice guy.'

Carly gave Velvet a speculative look, one Velvet chose to ignore. Jerard Daniels' behaviour had nothing to do with *her*, nothing at all. He seemed a bit on the explosive side to her anyway. It certainly didn't take much for him to lose his temper.

Greg stood up to leave. 'I'd better get back to work.'

'And I think I'll go to my room,' Velvet joined him. 'The sea air seems to knock me out.'

Greg grinned. 'It is pretty potent. If you're going to your room I might as well come with you, it just so happens that I have to go to the ninth floor myself.'

Velvet flushed, smiling her goodnight to Carly and Paul. 'See you in the morning.' She walked off, head held high. 'Do you really have to go to the ninth floor?' she asked Greg tightly as they travelled up in the lift together.

'Really,' he nodded. 'Hey, you didn't think I was moving in for the kill, did you?'

'I wasn't the only who thought it.' She knew Carly and Paul had had the same idea. In fact, that was the reason for her embarrassment.

'I have a complaint from the room a couple of doors

up from you,' he told her seriously. 'I have to look into it, soothe the situation down. Honest!'

She felt rather foolish now—conceited too. Greg had already told her he was on duty, she should have realised he wouldn't sneak off to her room, especially when he had already had one reprimand from Jerard Daniels today.

'I'm sorry,' she sighed. 'I'm just being silly.'

'Believe me, if I had the time . . .'

She laughed. 'Now you've spoilt it. I was just beginning to trust you,' she explained.

'I wouldn't want you to feel too safe,' he grinned. 'I'm not the sort of man who likes to make friends out of women.'

Velvet chuckled at his leering expression. 'If you're intending to ravish me——'

'Good evening, Mrs Dale. Boyd.'

All humour faded from Velvet at the sound of that harsh voice, her face suddenly pale as she turned to see Jerard Daniels blocking the corridor. 'Mr Daniels,' she returned in a stilted voice. 'Were you wanting to see me?'

He eyed Greg contemptuously, that contempt passing on to Velvet as his gaze returned to her. 'That was my intention, yes. But as you're busy . . .' He made to brush past her.

'I—er—I'm not busy,' she said hastily, remembering Faye Rogers and her decision to try and help the other woman. 'Greg was just going, weren't you, Greg?' She gave him a pleading look, aware of the interpretation Jerard Daniels had put on the situation—and she intended putting him straight about that at the earliest opportunity, like now!

'I—Oh yes,' Greg agreed eagerly, forgetting all about the complaint he had come up to deal with and stepping back into the lift.

The doors closed, leaving Velvet alone with Jerard Daniels. She licked her suddenly dry lips, subconsciously noticing how handsome he looked in the casual blue shirt and tight-fitting denims. 'I think I should tell you,' she began huskily, 'that Greg——'

'I'm not interested in what you intended doing in your room with one of my employees,' he cut in stonily. 'What you care to do with—friends of yours is none of my concern. Unless,' his gaze sharpened, 'Mr Boyd happens to be on duty, *then* I might make it my business. Is he?'

'Well, he——'

'Is he?'

'Yes! But——'

'Then I'll deal with him later,' he said grimly.

'Look, Mr Daniels, you have it all wrong. I——' she broke off as someone came out of a room farther up the corridor, giving them a curious look as he walked to the lift. 'Could we possibly discuss this in my room? she asked impatiently.

A speculative look came into those deep blue eyes. 'If you would prefer that.'

Velvet sighed. 'I wasn't suggesting anything but sorting out this muddle, Mr Daniels.' She unlocked her door, going inside to switch on the lights, opening the balcony doors in the heat of the evening. When she turned round it was to find Jerard Daniels seated in her one armchair, his long legs stretched out in front of him. 'Make yourself at home,' she said dryly.

'I am,' he returned equally dryly.

'Oh—Oh yes, of course.' She blushed at her stupidity, feeling ridiculously nervous with him looking so relaxed in the room that contained her bed.

'You were saying?' he prompted mockingly, his blue-eyed gaze running over her appearance with insolent appraisal.

It made Velvet feel hot all over to think that this man might have known her more intimately than any other man except Anthony.

'Velvet!' he snapped.

'I—Oh yes,' she licked her lips nervously. 'Greg wasn't with me, he was up here to answer a complaint.'

'Which he didn't do,' Jerard Daniels drawled.

'No. Well, he—You—you made him nervous, suddenly appearing like that!'

He sat forward. 'So now it's my fault,' he said tauntingly.

'What did you want to see me about, Mr Daniels?' she demanded to know, knowing now that she could never reason with this man about Faye Rogers.

He was on his feet in two seconds flat, his hands painfully grasping her upper arms. 'Don't "Mr Daniels" me one more time,' he bit out fiercely, 'or I swear I'll rape you where you stand!'

Velvet paled. 'Rape . . .?'

'Yes!' his teeth snapped together viciously. 'It would give me intense pleasure to remind you of all the things you've conveniently forgotten, to show you how well I know the pleasure of your body—and the pleasure I can give you.' His hands moved deliberately to the sensitive area just below her shoulder-blades, watching with satisfaction the shiver of exquisite pleasure that shot through every nerve in her body. 'You see?' he scorned. 'Every time you call me Mr Daniels you're challenging me to show you what else I know to do to make you squirm in ecstasy. And if you do it once more I swear I'll carry out my threat.'

She knew by the dangerous glitter in his eyes that he meant every word. She licked her lips nervously. 'I won't do it again,' she said shakily.

His gaze was fixed on the parted wetness of her mouth. 'Don't do that either!' he groaned. 'God, who am I kidding!' His arms tightened about her. 'I don't need an excuse to make love to you.' He pulled her roughly against him, his mouth covering hers.

It was exactly like the last time, the warm burning kisses that devoured and possessed her, the agony of memories she just couldn't bring to her conscious mind.

'God, Velvet,' he groaned against her lips, 'I'm going to *make* you admit to remembering me.'

'But I——'

He swung her up into his arms, walking over to the bed to deposit her on its softness before swiftly joining her, his leg over hers trapping her to the bed. 'Just lie back and enjoy it, Velvet,' he gave a taunting smile. 'Think of England if you have to,' he mocked before his mouth once more took possession of hers.

England! God, yes, England and Tony. She began to struggle, but Jerard just hurt her, all his weight now pressing her down into the bed, forcing her to accept the intimacy of his mouth, the rough caresses of his hands.

He wouldn't release her mouth from his, and Velvet felt the zip of her dress slide down her spine, the soft material pushed carelessly down to her waist. Her struggles were to no avail, and when she felt the fastening of her bra being undone, that lacy garment discarded to the floor, Jerard's fingertips on the rosy peaks of her breasts, she didn't want to struggle any more.

She gasped with pleasure, her head thrown back as Jerard's head moved down and his experienced lips claimed one nipple, the tip of his tongue causing excitement to ripple through her body.

'Do you remember me now?' he raised his head to rasp.

Her face contorted with pain and embarrassment. 'No,' she moaned, knowing she didn't tell the whole truth. She *did* remember being kissed like this before, she just didn't know when; by whom was obvious. 'I—Perhaps you could tell me——'

'I'm *showing* you,' he snapped, suddenly moving off the bed to look down at her with open contempt. 'Maybe it's as well your husband died when he did,' his mouth twisted. 'You probably can't even remember the way he made love either.'

She went deathly white. She *didn't* remember Anthony's lovemaking. But this man didn't know the reason for that, couldn't even begin to imagine why she didn't even remember Anthony being her husband.

She bit her lip. 'I wish you would let me explain——'

'There's nothing to explain,' he dismissed harshly. 'You once again seduced me into your bed——'

She sat up indignantly, hastily pulling her gown up over her bare breasts. '*I* seduced *you*?' she exclaimed. 'Well, I like that!'

'So do I,' he mocked harshly. 'Which is why I have to get out of here.'

Velvet frowned as he walked to the door. 'Was—this the reason you came down here?' she choked.

He gave a derisive smile. 'No. Believe it or not I came down to apologise for my behaviour earlier. Vicki assures me that I certainly "pulled a face" at you.'

Her face softened as she thought of the little girl. 'How is she now?'

'Asleep,' he said huskily. 'Maybe I should apologise for what happened just now too, but as I enjoyed every minute of it I would only be lying if I said I wished it hadn't happened. You're as beautiful as ever, Velvet. I thought after all this time that I must have imagined the taste and feel of you—if anything I'd forgotten some of your beauty.' He shook his head. 'I wish—I wish you'd still loved me, Velvet.' He closed the door quietly behind him as he left.

She collapsed back on the bed, staring up at the ceiling, still quivering from Jerard's caresses. Her hand trembled as she pushed her hair back from her face, a curious ache in the region of her stomach, a longing for—for——

She suddenly sprang up from the bed, pushing these tortuous thoughts to the back of her mind, knowing her body was aflame with what her mind refused to remember. Her body remembered Jerard Daniels, it ached for him, each nerve alive and waiting, waiting . . .

Well, it would wait for ever! Jerard Daniels might have caught her unawares just now, but that would never happen again, that scene on her bed would *never* happen again.

She went out on to her balcony; the view from her ninth floor window was quite spectacular—the ocean looked dark and beautiful, the clear moonlight picking out the white crests of the waves before they crashed against the golden sand. The palm trees gently swayed in the breeze, the air was warm even at this time of night.

What had happened between Jerard Daniels and herself just now couldn't really mean anything, not emotionally mean anything. She had just been a normal young woman responding to a yearning that hadn't been satisfied since Anthony died, a yearning she hadn't even realised existed.

But of course it existed! She was twenty-two, not ninety-two, and she had a need to be loved and made love to like any other healthy woman of that age. Paul had been trying to tell her that earlier, and she hadn't wanted to listen to him. How silly she must have sounded when she told them Tony was all she needed! Of course she needed more than that, needed a man in her life. But Jerard Daniels couldn't be that man, not with the past hanging between them like a threatening shadow.

She sighed, going back into her room and closing the

doors to begin preparing for bed. A cold shower was supposed to be good for what she was suffering from—or did that only apply to men? Oh well, it was worth a try. If she didn't calm down, couldn't calm this mad excitement in her veins, then she was never going to get to sleep tonight.

She did sleep, eventually, although it wasn't until she had relived every touch, every kiss Jerard Daniels had given her. She experienced them again and again in her mind, her sleep one of erotic dreams, the promised loving fulfilled. She was in such a pleasant state of euphoria that when the telephone rang in her dream and she picked it up to hear Jerard's voice on the other end of the line she wasn't in the least surprised or dismayed.

'Hello, darling,' she greeted dreamily.

'Darling?' he echoed sharply. 'This is Jerard,' he explained tersely.

'Yes, I know,' she said softly.

'Velvet! Velvet, are you awake?' he rasped.

The fog cleared from her numbed brain, only to realise that she was actually talking to Jerard Daniels on the telephone. 'I—You—What time is it?'

'Three o'clock in the morning,' he growled. 'Were they pleasant dreams?' he asked tauntingly.

'Yes. I mean—No. I didn't have any dreams!' she denied heatedly.

'I'll bet,' he drawled. 'Velvet, I need you.'

She swallowed hard. 'I—I beg your pardon?' The dreams seemed so vivid, so real, that for a moment she was having trouble distinguishing them from reality.

'Not for my own sake,' he dismissed coldly. 'It's Vicki. She's damn near hysteria. She woke up screaming, now she just keeps crying and asking for you.'

'For me? But——'

'She needs you, Velvet.'

'Of course,' she threw back the sheet, swinging her

legs to the floor. 'I'll come up immediately.'

'Velvet!' He just caught her before she put the telephone down. 'Take the time to dress first, hmm?' he suggested tautly.

'I was going to!' she said indignantly.

'I hope so. It's my daughter you're coming up here to help, not me.'

'How could I help—Oh!' She slammed the telephone down as she realised in what way he was implying she could help him.

Their personal differences, or mutual attraction, had to be put to one side. Vicki was the one who counted now, the one they had to concern themselves with.

She was to wish she hadn't loved Vicki on sight at a later date, although she had no way of knowing that now. If she had known she might have ignored the first cry for help—although she doubted it.

Vicki looked a sorry sight when Jerard let Velvet into his apartment, a small figure dressed in a cotton flowered nightgown, her hair wild across the pillow, her face red and swollen from the tears she had shed. But she was quiet now, staring straight ahead, her eyes a dull uninterested blue.

Velvet frowned at Jerard. 'What happened?' she whispered.

He was pale, obviously deeply distressed by his daughter's condition. 'Shortly after I called you she went like this.' He ran a hand through his already tousled dark hair, seeming to have hastily pulled on denims and a shirt, the shirt tucked loosely into the waistband of the denims but not a single button fastened, his tanned chest covered with a mat of fine dark hair.

Velvet hastily looked away from the sensuality of him, her dreams still vivid in her mind. Her attention returned to Vicki with effort. 'Has she been like this before?'

'Not since my wife died,' he replied distractedly.

She sighed. 'It was the mention of the hospital.'

He frowned. 'Hospital?'

'Greg took Miss Rogers to the hospital. It seemed to upset Vicki, which was why I took her for an ice-cream before coming back here.' She brushed past him into the bedroom. 'Vicki?' she prompted huskily.

Pained blue eyes were turned on her, then the cotton nightgown-clad figure flew across the room to launch itself into her arms. 'Velvet!' Vicki sobbed. 'Oh, Velvet, I thought you wouldn't come! I thought you'd gone away like Faye did, like—like Mummy did,' she trembled.

'Faye hasn't gone away,' she smoothed Vicki's hair back from her heated forehead. 'She's just getting better. And Mummy had to go away, poppet. Mummies sometimes have to do that.' She sat down in the bedroom chair, Vicki cradled in her lap.

'But why?'

Velvet looked up at Jerard, sure that this whole situation must be very painful for him. She looked down at Vicki; the little girl's sobs were quietening now. 'Mummy was ill, and she—she hurt, very badly.' She bit her lip, never having to cope with something like this before. 'You didn't really want Mummy to hurt any more, did you?'

'No . . .'

'And she isn't, not now.'

'But she went away!'

'Yes, but—but she left you your daddy, and your daddy loves you very much.'

Vicki nodded, her eyes starting to droop tiredly. 'I love Daddy, too.' Her thin arms crept up about Velvet's neck. 'And I love you. You won't go away, will you, Velvet?'

'No, poppet,' her voice was husky, 'I'll stay here until you go to sleep.'

Vicki instantly stiffened. 'No, I mean you won't go away, ever.'

Velvet looked to Jerard for help, relieved when he came down on his haunches in front of his daughter.

He held her hand in his, smoothing his thumb across the back of it. 'Vicki,' he began softly, 'Velvet has her own little boy to go home to.'

Blue eyes so like her father's opened wide. 'She does?'

'Yes,' he nodded. 'And he's only a little baby, so he needs her more than you do.'

'Oh.'

'You do understand, Vicki?' he smiled gently.

'I—I think so,' she nodded sleepily.

Velvet stood up, Vicki still in her arms, and placed the thin little body back into the single bed, sitting down beside her as she clutched at her hand. 'I'll stay right here until you're asleep,' she assured her. 'Why don't you go into the other room?' she spoke softly to Jerard. 'There's no point in both of us sitting here.' And he looked in need of a drink.

'No,' he agreed huskily, coming over to kiss his daughter affectionately on the forehead. ' 'Night, darling.'

' 'Night, Daddy.' Her arms clung around his throat. 'I'm sorry if I was a—a nuisance.'

'You're never a nuisance,' he told her firmly.

'But I made you get Velvet—and everything.'

'It doesn't matter,' he kissed her again, infinitely gentle with the person who meant the most to him. 'Go to sleep now,' he encouraged.

She relaxed back on the pillows, asleep even before her arms slipped from around his throat. He tucked the blankets more firmly about her, gazing down at her with a haggard expression.

'Will she be all right now?' Velvet asked him once they were in the lounge.

He gave a deep sigh. 'I hope so.' He poured himself out some whisky. 'Would you like one?' He swallowed all the fiery liquid in one gulp.

'No, thank you,' she shook her head.

Jerard slumped down in an armchair. 'She hasn't been as bad as that since her mother died. God, that Rogers woman has a lot to answer for!' His expression was savage.

'She couldn't help falling,' Velvet pointed out reasonably.

He drew a ragged breath. 'No, I suppose not.'

'I—Well, I'd better be going now,' and she turned, graceful even in denims and red cotton sun-top.

'No!' his protest stopped her, and she turned slowly. 'Stay for a while,' he pleaded.

He looked ill, grey beneath the tan, deep lines of weariness beside his eyes. Velvet's heart softened towards him. 'Just for a few minutes,' she agreed softly, and sat down, sensing his need not to be alone.

'Are you sure you wouldn't like a drink?' he asked after several minutes of companionable silence.

'Very sure,' she nodded. 'Although I wouldn't mind a cup of coffee. Still,' she shrugged, 'it doesn't matter.'

'But it does matter.' Jerard stood up, pulling her to her feet and taking her into a kitchen. 'Help yourself,' he opened the cupboard containing the makings of a cup of coffee.

'I didn't realise,' she put the coffee on to percolate. 'I thought I'd have to send down for some,' she explained with a blush.

His mouth twisted, as he replenished his whisky glass. 'Something you didn't intend doing, not when it would mean letting my staff know you're up here with me at four o'clock in the morning.'

She looked down at her hands. 'No.'

'The kitchen is new, Velvet,' he taunted. 'You

probably remember it as a bedroom.'

Her head went back in shock. '*I* remember it as a bedroom?'

His mouth set in a thin line. 'Something else you've forgotten?' he rasped, swallowing the remainder of his whisky.

She bit her lip, her bottom lip trembling vulnerably. 'I've been here before?' she asked in distress; she had never felt so lost before, not even when Anthony had died.

Jerard turned on his heel and walked out of the room. Velvet followed him slowly, the coffee forgotten, looking about the apartment with new eyes. She looked at Jerard, seeing the contempt in his face.

'You'd better go, Velvet,' he snapped, 'before I finally lose my temper with you.'

Finally? What had he been doing since they first met? 'I want to explain to you——'

'Explain what, for God's sake?' he exploded. 'That you chose to forget me as soon as you had your lawyer's ring on your finger? I realise now that I was just a last fling for you. After all, every girl likes one lover before she settles down with her husband. I should have realised I was yours,' he added disgustedly. 'God, I was thirty-seven then, I should have realised a twenty-year-old girl wouldn't seriously be interested in me.'

He had to be joking! He was the sort of man who would have women, of all ages, interested in him when he was seventy. He would never lose his harsh good looks, the muscled straightness of his body. Yes, women would always find him attractive—as she did.

'Mr—Jerard,' she hastily amended as she remembered his threat of earlier, knowing by the twist of his lips that he too recalled it. She licked her lips, hurriedly stopping that too as she remembered how provocative he found it. She set her mouth in a straight line, her gaze unflinching as she looked at him. 'I want to tell you why everything you tell me about the past is a mystery to me,' she said firmly, her tone very positive.

'Strange,' he taunted. 'Nothing about you is a mystery to me.'

Her eyes flashed darkly brown. 'Will you listen to me!' she raised her voice, determined he was going to hear her out, even if it took the few brief hours left until morning!

'Go ahead,' he shrugged uninterestedly, leaning back with his eyes closed.

Velvet glared at him. If he dared to fall asleep . . .! 'Are you listening?' she demanded angrily.

'Avidly.' He made himself more comfortable, his eyes still closed.

She sighed her frustration. How could she talk to a man who to all intents and purposes was fast asleep! 'Jerard——'

'Okay, okay,' he sighed, sitting up, a bored expression on his face. 'Go ahead.'

A bored listener was better than no listener at all, so she began to tell him of that year she had no memory of, haltingly at first, and then in a rush as she knew she had the whole of his attention, and his eyes narrowed as he listened.

'So there you have it,' she finished with a shrug. 'The doctors said it could all come back, but then again it may just remain a—a blank.' She looked at him searchingly.

Jerard didn't say anything, as the seconds stretched into minutes, and still he continued to look at her, his eyes becoming colder and colder by the minute. Finally he stood up, his face a harsh mask. 'Very convenient,' he drawled insultingly. 'But if I'd wanted to listen to a fairy story I could have got you to read one out of Vicki's books. Now, if you don't mind, I'd like to get a couple of hours' sleep.' He turned his back on her.

It was such a definite snub that it couldn't be ignored. 'You don't believe me,' Velvet choked. He was the only person outside her family who had ever been told her secret, and he didn't believe a word of it!

He turned, his expression contemptuous. 'Was I supposed to?' he scorned. 'Credit me with some sense, Velvet. It's like something out of a soap-opera,' he derided.

Her bottom lip trembled emotionally. 'But it's the truth!'

'Maybe the truth as you like to see it. Was your marriage to Anthony Dale such a disaster that you prefer to claim you've forgotten it?' his voice was thick with sarcasm.

She winced as if he had physically struck her. 'My marriage to Anthony wasn't a disaster at all,' she denied heatedly.

Jerard's mouth twisted derisively. 'I thought you couldn't remember it,' he taunted.

'I can't,' she flushed deeply.

'Then how do you know it was a success?'

'My brother——'

'Ah yes, Simon.'

She gasped. 'You know my brother?'

Jerard shook his head. 'Only what you've told me about him.'

'I—I talked about Simon?'

Jerard nodded. 'And his wife, Janice.'

It was very disconcerting that this man should know so much about her when she knew next to nothing about him. 'Well, Simon told me I was happy with Anthony,' she defended.

'And how would he know that?'

'Well, I—It was obvious!'

'Believe me, nothing is that obvious.'

'But I was happy with him,' she declared stubbornly. 'I—We—I have Tony to prove how happy I was with Anthony.'

'And I have Vicki to prove how happy I was with Tina,' Jerard mocked. 'And we both know I was never that.'

'You weren't?' she blinked, taking Tina to be his wife.

'For God's sake, Velvet,' he snapped, 'you've taken this farce far enough. You've shown me quite plainly that you aren't interested in carrying on where we left off two years ago. There's no need to pretend that either of us loved our spouses.'

'I loved Anthony!'

'Like hell you did!'

Tears flooded her eyes. 'But I did.'

'As a child might love a friend maybe, or as a sister might love an adored older brother, but not as anything else, not as a lover, not like you loved me—or like I *thought* you loved me,' he amended harshly. 'But that's over with now, Velvet, the dream turned out to be just that. You aren't the girl I fell in love with, that girl would never use such a feeble story to hide from the fact that she loved me enough to spend a stolen week with me, a week when we hardly ventured out of this apartment, a week when we made love until we were dizzy with it, a week when I thought you'd given yourself to me so completely that not even the passage of time could part us. No, you aren't that girl,' he added quietly. 'She had more guts in her little finger than you have in the whole of that beautiful body you take such pride in.'

His last insults passed over her head. 'I stayed with you for a whole week?' she swallowed hard.

'Yes,' he snapped confirmation.

Oh heavens, it was worse than she had thought. When

Jerard claimed they had been lovers she had imagined it had been an impulsive one night in a stranger's arms. But a week! God, it was a lifetime—and it could hardly be called impulsive! She wished she knew exactly what had happened that week—beside the fact that they seemed to have made love constantly!

'I—I don't know what to say,' she mumbled dazedly, totally confused by what Jerard had just told her.

'Don't say anything,' he dismissed harshly. 'Just don't ever repeat that drivel to me again. If you would rather forget the time we shared together then consider it forgotten—by both of us,' he added grimly. 'As far as I'm concerned you're a stranger, anyway.'

Velvet flinched, wishing in some way she could make him believe her. 'Jerard——'

'Goodnight, Velvet,' he cut in firmly. 'I'm grateful for your help with Vicki,' the words seemed to be forced out of him, 'but I won't bother you again.'

'And if Vicki should need me?'

His face hardened. 'We'll deal with that when—and if—it happens.' His tone left her in no doubt as to his feelings on the matter.

She stumbled out of the apartment and went back up to her own room. Well, she had told Jerard the truth and he hadn't believed her, there was nothing else she could do—except cry herself to sleep. And she did that, somehow feeling hurt and confused by Jerard's treatment of her.

CHAPTER FOUR

VELVET slept in late the next morning, waking up after ten, wondering why Carly or Paul hadn't come to her room and demanded her presence for work on the beach. She soon found out why they hadn't!

'Daniels called me early this morning,' Paul muttered, as she joined him and Carly by the pool. 'He said you didn't leave him until four-thirty this morning, so you'd need to rest.'

Colour flamed in her cheeks. 'Did he explain why I was in his apartment until four-thirty this morning?'

Paul looked mocking. 'No, and I didn't ask him.'

'I went to see Vicki,' she defended indignantly. Jerard had done this deliberately!

'Of course you did,' Paul nodded.

'But I did!'

'I just agreed, didn't I?' he taunted.

She frowned. 'It was the *way* you agreed.'

Carly giggled. 'Well, really, Velvet, that was a pretty feeble excuse. His little girl must have been in bed hours by that time of morning.'

'She had, but she woke up, and she wanted me. She— she seems to have taken to me,' Velvet revealed awkwardly.

'Like her father,' Paul teased. 'All right, all right, there's no need to get violent,' he said at her furious expression. 'So you and Jerard Daniels didn't so much as hold hands last night.'

Velvet blushed as she remembered just how intimately Jerard had touched her, still confused by her own reaction to those caresses, although luckily they hadn't haunted her dreams the second time she went to bed.

Paul was watching her closely. 'On second thoughts,' he said slowly, 'maybe he did—and a lot more besides, by the look on your face.'

'Paul——'

'You're embarrassing her again,' Carly told him. 'Let's go for a swim and leave her to calm down.'

'I'm going back inside,' Velvet told them crossly. 'I take it we aren't working today?'

'No.' Paul stood up, very lean and attractive in navy blue swimming trunks. 'We've nearly finished, anyway.'

'Does that mean we can go home soon?' Velvet asked hopefully.

He nodded. 'We're booked on a plane to England in two days.'

'Good!' She made no effort to hide her pleasure in that arrangement.

'Missing Tony?' Carly sympathised.

'Too much to want to do this again in a hurry,' she nodded. 'I think I'll go and get myself some breakfast.'

'Next time I should make Daniels provide that,' Paul teased. 'It's the usual practice.'

Her answer was to push him into the pool, watching with satisfaction as he came up spluttering.

'Good for you!' Carly chuckled, diving smoothly into the water to join her boy-friend.

Velvet was still smiling as she drank her coffee and ate her toast, the smile broadening as Greg joined her a few minutes later.

He pulled out a chair and sat down. 'You're still in one piece, then?' he gave a rueful grin.

She nodded. 'And you?'

'Mm. I've had a bit more of my tail chewed off, but I'm otherwise unscathed.'

'I'm sorry about that.' Her smile faded.

'It wasn't your fault.' He touched her hand.

She knew that it was. If Jerard hadn't come down to see her he would never have seen Greg. But Greg seemed prepared to forget it, and so must she. 'Did you ever see to that complaint?'

He gave a rueful smile. 'Eventually—after they'd complained that I hadn't seen to the first complaint.'

'Oh dear!' Velvet burst out laughing, then her humour faded as she saw Jerard Daniels and Vicki standing in the doorway of the dining-room. She looked away. 'Are you on duty, Greg?' she asked softly.

'Sure. But why—Oh no!' he groaned, seeing Jerard too. 'Not again!' He put his face in his hands.

Velvet knew how he felt, she was beginning to feel rather haunted by Jerard herself. 'Maybe if you just get up and leave he won't say anything,' she suggested hopefully. 'After all, you have to be pleasant to the guests.'

'But not one guest in particular,' Greg grimaced. 'Oh well, here goes.' He stood up, walking calmly to the door. 'Sir,' he greeted politely.

'Boyd,' Jerard nodded curtly.

Velvet felt the tension leave her as Greg managed to escape without the verbal slaughtering he had been expecting, and turned back to her coffee, still deeply aware of Jerard being somewhere in the room.

'Can I ask her now, Daddy?' Vicki could be heard asking excitedly.

'Vicki, I told you——'

'Oh, *please*, Daddy!' she pleaded.

Whatever it was the little girl wanted Velvet didn't see how her father could hold out against her, she knew she wouldn't be able to.

'Okay,' he murmured agreement. 'But no pressurising,' he warned.

Vicki appeared beside Velvet's table, jumping up and down in her excitement. No sign of her distress of last night was now evident in her animated face, and her shorts and top were as casual as Velvet's own.

'Hello,' Velvet greeted her with a smile.

'Hello,' Vicki returned, suddenly shy.

'Would you like to join me?' Velvet invited, at the same time sensing Jerard's presence close by. A curious sensation fluttered down her spine, and she looked up into his hard blue eyes as he came to stand behind Vicki, the cream shirt and brown trousers showing the taut outline of his body.

He didn't approve of Vicki talking to her, it was there in every hard line of his body, and Velvet's hackles rose in indignation. Just who did he think he was anyway!

'Daddy and I ate breakfast upstairs,' Vicki told her in her serious little voice.

'Oh. Well, would you like some fruit juice?' She indicated the jug of fresh orange juice on the table.

'Yes, please.' Vicki gave a wide grin and perched herself on one of the chairs.

Velvet looked calmly up at Jerard Daniels as he still loomed over them. 'Would you like some?' she asked him casually, pouring Vicki's into a glass.

The set of his mouth showed his disgust. 'Not for me,' he refused calmly enough.

'Would you like to sit down?' she invited, not at all daunted by his attitude.

'No——'

'Oh, sit down, Daddy!' Vicki's nose came out of the glass long enough for her to request, a ring of orange around her top lip. 'I haven't asked Velvet yet, and besides, I have to drink my orange juice.'

He did so with ill-grace, his thigh momentarily touching Velvet's, and her bare skin tingled from the contact. She was wearing yellow silky shorts and matching top, prepared for the heat of the day, although now she wished she had worn something else, something that didn't make her feel quite so naked.

She looked at Vicki, pointedly ignoring Jerard. 'Haven't asked me what, poppet?'

The little girl put down her empty glass. 'I—We—Daddy!' she looked to her father for help.

His expression was stern. 'It was your idea, Vicki.'

'Yes, but—Daddy, please!' once again she used that heartrending tone Velvet had thought hard to resist.

'Very well.' Jerard obviously had trouble resisting it too. 'Vicki and I are driving down to Orlando this afternoon,' he told Velvet stiffly.

She frowned. 'Yes?'

He gave her an impatient look. 'To Disneyworld.'

'Yes?' She still frowned, surprised by his need to tell her of his movements.

'We—I want you to come with us,' Vicki burst out eagerly.

'Oh no. No, I——'

'Oh please,' Vicki pleaded. 'It will be such fun with the three of us!'

Velvet looked at Jerard for help, but his expression remained impassive, telling her more clearly than any words could do that he wanted no part of her refusal. He probably didn't want to get the blame for it later. And she couldn't really blame him, no one would wish a sulky child upon themselves unless they had to.

But he knew she had to refuse, damn him! He should never have allowed Vicki to ask her. The fact that he hadn't exactly encouraged his daughter slipped Velvet's mind for the moment, deliberately so if she cared to probe into it. She enjoyed being able to be angry with him, it gave her an excuse to dislike him. Although after the way he had disbelieved her last night she wasn't sure she needed an excuse!

'I'm afraid I can't join you, Vicki.' She instantly felt guilty as she saw the disappointment the little girl was unable to hide. 'I really can't,' she said contritely. 'I'm here to work, and——'

'But you work for Daddy!' Vicki blinked back the tears, her bottom lip trembling emotionally. 'Daddy, you'll let Velvet have time off to come with us, won't you?'

'I don't think she wants to——'

'It isn't that,' Velvet cut in sharply, shooting Jerard a sharp look. He didn't have to make this any worse than it was. 'Try to understand, Vicki,' her expression softened as she looked at the little girl. 'I'm here to work, and if I take time off I won't be finished in time to catch my plane home the day after tomorrow. And my little boy is depending on my getting home then. I can't let him down, Vicki.'

The little girl's face crumpled and she burst into tears, getting noisily down from the chair to run sobbing out of the room.

Velvet stood up. 'Vicki——'

'It's all right,' Jerard held her back from running after his daughter. 'Leave her,' he ordered curtly. 'She'll only go up to the suite.'

'But I——'

'I said leave her, Velvet.'

She glared at him angrily. 'I heard what you said, but I can't just leave her like that. I have to go after her.'

'And do what?' his mouth twisted.

'Well, I—I——'

'Are you going to agree to come to Disneyworld with us?'

'You know I can't——'

'Then leave her.'

'You know I can't go,' she babbled out her guilt about disappointing the child, feeling awful about it. 'I have to finish my work——'

'Paul tells me he's more or less finished with you,'

Jerard cut in. 'That he can take the remainder of the shots back in his studio in London.'

Velvet gasped. 'You asked him?'

'It came up in the conversation——'

'I'll bet it did!' she said fiercely. 'In the same conversation you implied I had spent the night with you, I suppose?'

His mouth quirked with humour. 'Did I do that?'

'You know you did!' she accused heatedly. 'Carly and Paul both have the idea that I slept with you last night.'

It was as if a shutter had come down; his eyes were once more cold, his expression remote. 'Then they're both wrong,' he rasped.

'I know that——'

'Then stop making a damned issue out of it!' He stood up. 'I'm going up to Vicki now.'

She grasped his arm before he could move away. 'I— Did you really mean it about my not having any more work to do?'

Jerard's eyes narrowed. 'Yes.'

She drew a deep breath. 'Then I'll come to Disneyworld,' she said in a rush.

He scowled heavily. 'Wouldn't you rather try and get an earlier flight home?'

She would, of course she would. But she wasn't really expected back for another two days. Tony would be fine with Simon and Janice, and at the moment Vicki seemed to need her more.

'Vicki will get over it,' Jerard told her in a cold voice.

'Will she?' Velvet asked shrilly. 'Don't you think she's having to "get over" rather a lot lately? First her mother's death, then Miss Roger's accident, and now my apparent defection.'

'And if she becomes attached to you, what then?'

'I—We can cross that bridge when we get to it—if we get to it,' she added pointedly.

'We will,' he sighed. 'She likes you now, and very soon she's going to love you. And when that happens . . .'

'It may not.'

'It will,' he said with certainty. 'And when it does we're going to be in one hell of a mess.'

'I think you're exaggerating,' Velvet said stubbornly.

'Do you?' his expression was glacial. 'You'll soon see I'm not. All right, Mrs Dale, pack a few things and come with us. But if you don't like the way this situation develops, don't blame me.'

'I won't,' she answered vaguely, frowning. 'Did you say pack a few things?'

'I did,' he nodded.

'I—We'll be staying overnight?'

'We will.'

'Oh, but I—I didn't realise that,' she groaned.

'It takes almost four hours to get to Orlando from here,' he explained patiently. 'I intend driving up this afternoon, staying overnight at my hotel there, and then letting Vicki have all day at Disneyworld tomorrow. She can be sleeping in the back during our drive here in the evening. Changed your mind?' he quirked a mocking eyebrow.

Velvet flushed her resentment. 'No. Those arrangements will suit me just fine.'

'All right,' he sighed. 'Just remember, it was your decision.'

'I'll remember,' she snapped.

The look on Vicki's face when they told her Velvet was going with them after all was all that she needed to tell her she had made the right decision. Trying to convince Paul and Carly that she was going merely for Vicki's sake was something else. She gave up in the end, and hurried to her room to pack an overnight case.

Jerrard kept a Ferrari at the hotel, and Vicki was

bouncing up and down on the back seat when Velvet met them outside later that afternoon.

'You'll sit in the front with me,' Jerard instructed as she went to get in the back.

'I would rather——'

'In the front!' He got out of the car to stow her case in the boot.

Velvet took advantage of his momentary absence to slip into the back beside Vicki, grinning conspiratorially at the little girl. Vicki grinned back, and her hand crept into Velvet's.

Jerard's face darkened as he turned in his seat to look at her. 'Out!' he ordered grimly.

'But I——'

'I said you were to sit in the front,' he said coldly. 'And that's where you'll sit.'

Velvet felt foolish getting out and then getting back in—to the front seat this time. She didn't know why Jerard had to make such an issue about where she sat, she would have been infinitely more comfortable sitting beside Vicki. But maybe that was the idea; Jerard hadn't exactly encouraged her to come on this trip with them, so perhaps he didn't intend that she should be 'comfortable'.

'You're getting a persecution complex,' he remarked dryly as they set out on the long drive to Orlando.

She blinked up at him. 'I——'

He gave her a sideways glance. 'That was your idea, wasn't it?' he taunted.

'I—No, of course not,' she flushed.

'Liar,' he mocked. 'Do you have more room in the front?' he asked casually.

'Yes. But——'

'Point proved,' he said dryly.

'Daddy's *always* right.' Vicki sat forward to lean her arms on the back of their seats.

His mouth quirked with humour. 'Not always, darling,' he drawled.

'Oh, but you are,' she insisted guilelessly.

'I wasn't right about Velvet coming with us today.'

'No,' his daughter agreed slowly. 'But I'm glad she has.'

'So am I,' Jerard said softly.

'You are?' Velvet looked at him sharply, searching for sarcasm in the hard planes of his face.

'Of course,' he taunted. 'You can help keep Vicki occupied.'

'I intended doing that anyway,' she snapped resentfully. 'That was the reason I sat in the back.'

He quirked one eyebrow. 'Not to avoid being near me?'

'Certainly not,' she told him waspishly. 'Why should I need to do that?'

He shrugged. 'Why indeed?'

'Don't you like my daddy?' Vicki asked innocently.

'That isn't the sort of question to ask anyone,' her father told her sternly. 'It isn't polite.'

'Why?'

'It just isn't.'

'But why isn't it?'

Jerard sighed. 'We've had this conversation before, Vicki. Don't keep answering a reply to a question with another one.'

'Wh—Sorry. I just wondered if Velvet liked you, that was all,' she said sulkily.

'And I told you not to ask questions like that.'

'I don't mind,' Velvet cut in. 'Yes, I like your daddy, Vicki,' and strangely enough she did, although she wished he would believe her about the past.

'He likes you too, I can tell,' Vicki said smugly.

'Can you indeed, young lady?' Jerard couldn't keep the amusement out of his voice.

'Oh yes,' she nodded seriously. 'You've stopped pulling face—er—scowling at her.'

Velvet hadn't noticed! She thought by the amused smirk on Jerard's face that he hadn't either.

'Sit back, Vicki,' he ordered, 'and stop asking personal questions.'

His daughter pouted. 'But I wanted to know about Velvet's little boy.'

His expression hardened. 'Maybe Velvet doesn't want to talk about him.'

He didn't want her to, that much was obvious. 'I don't mind,' she answered abruptly. 'I'll talk to Vicki, Mr Daniels, while you concentrate on your driving.'

'I can talk and drive at the same time,' he rasped. 'And last night you called me Jerard.'

'And this morning you called me Mrs Dale,' she reminded tautly.

'So I did,' he sighed. 'Okay, this trip we're Jerard and Velvet. All right?'

'That's fine by me.' She turned away from him. 'What did you want to know about Tony?' Her voice softened as she spoke to Vicki.

'Is that your little boy's name?' she asked eagerly.

'Mm,' she nodded, smiling.

'How old is he?'

'Just over a year.'

Vicki grinned. 'I bet he's cute.'

'Well, I think so,' she laughed.

'Does he look like you?'

Velvet was aware of Jerard listening very closely to this conversation, and she did her best to ignore him, although it wasn't easy. 'Quite a bit,' she nodded. 'He has blond curly hair and huge brown eyes.'

'Doesn't he look anything like his father?' Jerard cut in.

'He has his serious nature,' she answered, at once on the defensive.

'Not a lot to leave his son,' he drawled sneeringly.

'He left his love too,' she flared. 'I'll make sure Tony knows all about what a wonderful man his father was.'

'Did Tony's daddy go away?' Vicki asked in a puzzled voice.

'He—he died, Vicki,' Velvet revealed reluctantly. The poor little girl was going to think mummies and daddies died all the time!

Vicki frowned. 'So Tony doesn't have a daddy?'

'No . . .'

'Mm,' the little girl said thoughtfully. 'Do you want to play I-Spy, Velvet?' she asked suddenly.

She saw Jerard's mouth twitch out of the corner of her eye. 'Why don't we all play?' she suggested with saccharine sweetness.

Vicki grimaced. 'Daddy's too good at it, he always wins.'

'Then you and I will play against him. I think that's fair, don't you?' she asked him.

'Very fair,' he nodded, his eyes twinkling with enjoyment. 'But no cheating.'

'We don't cheat, do we, Vicki?' she gasped.

'My daughter does,' Jerard said tongue-in-cheek. 'Mainly because she can't spell.'

Vicki giggled. 'It's more fun when you play it my way.'

'Not when you spell knee with an N,' her father derided.

Velvet laughed. 'Did you really do that?'

'Yes,' Vicki giggled. 'Daddy was trying to guess it for *ages*.'

For the next half an hour they played I-Spy, the two girls narrowly beating Jerard, although Velvet had the idea he had let them win. Vicki was ecstatic about the victory, sitting on the back seat with a huge grin on her face.

'That was nice,' Velvet said softly, too softly for Vicki to hear.

'I have been known to be nice on occasion,' Jerard drawled equally as softly. 'Although I very rarely allow anyone to win but myself.'

She looked at him sharply, sensing a warning. His expression remained bland. 'Will we be eating soon or will we wait until we get to Orlando?' she changed the subject, unwilling to start an argument with Jerard in front of the sensitive child Vicki undoubtedly was.

'Now, Daddy,' Vicki chimed in from behind. 'Let's eat now.'

'Hamburgers and french-fries, I suppose?' he grimaced.

'Yes, please,' she smiled her satisfaction.

'She lives on them whenever we're in America,' he explained to Velvet.

'Do you visit America a lot?' she asked interestedly.

'Not for some time,' he answered stiltedly. 'I come here as seldom as possible—at least, I did in the past. Now it seems the reason for my reluctance no longer exists.'

Colour flamed in her cheeks, his meaning clear to her. She had no appetite for the food he ordered for her, although he and Vicki didn't seem to share her lack of appetite, and both of them had a dessert too.

The drive itself was boring, a single straight road that led directly to Orlando. It was a monotonous journey, mile after mile of straight white road, hour after hour of travelling. It came as no surprise to Velvet that Vicki fell asleep half way.

'Did she continue to sleep last night?' she asked Jerard.

'Yes. Although she asked for you as soon as she woke up. I can't understand it,' he said tersely. 'She doesn't usually take to—strangers.'

She flinched, for some reason taking exception to being called a stranger. Although she didn't know why she did, because that was exactly what she was.

'I like her too,' she said huskily.

'Well, don't like her too much,' he advised harshly. 'I don't want a hysterical child on my hands once you've gone.'

She bit her lip. 'There's something I've been meaning to ask you,' she said slowly.

'Yes?'

His abrupt tone wasn't very encouraging, but she just had to ask him this next question. 'Your wife,' she began hesitantly. 'You were married when I—when we——'

'And if I was?' he rasped.

'Well, I—I—Oh God!' she groaned. 'I just find it impossible to believe I was involved with a married man.'

'Maybe I didn't tell you I was married.'

Her expression brightened. 'Didn't you? Is that the way it happened?'

'It "happened" because you wanted me and I wanted you,' he scorned. 'No other reason.'

'But you said we were in love!'

'At the time I thought we were, now I think it was just that other four-letter word beginning with L—lust,' he derided. 'That's a much more common reason for what we did.'

'Lust doesn't last for years,' she said heatedly. 'And you—you still loved me when we met again for the first time.'

'Did I?' he drawled.

'You know you did,' Velvet snapped.

'Maybe,' he conceded. 'But I'm over it now.'

She bit her lip, looking down at her hands. 'Why did we break up?'

Jerard sighed angrily. 'You might find it amusing to play this little game, Velvet, but it just sickens me. You know damn well we didn't break up. I had to take over the family business when my father died, and then we found out that Tina was ill, possibly dying. By the time I had the whole sorry mess sorted out you were Mrs Anthony Dale.'

Velvet had gone very white. 'That's what happened?'

'You know it is,' he said grimly.

'But if you were married——'

'I wasn't! You know damn well that in any sense of the word I wasn't,' he said more calmly. 'Tina and I had been separated a long time before I even met you.'

Her relief was immense. He hadn't been living with his wife when she had known him! Their past relationship didn't seem quite so bad now, although she still found it unnerving to think she and this man had been lovers.

'That makes you feel better, hmm?' he scorned. 'Have you forgotten you were engaged at the time?'

She had forgotten, and he knew she had; his sarcasm was obvious. And no wonder, she had been feeling smug with herself. Now she was feeling guilty again, totally unsure of herself, as only this man could make her feel.

Vicki woke up at that moment. 'Are we nearly there, Daddy?' she asked sleepily.

'Nearly.' His voice softened as he spoke to his daughter.

'Ooh, I can't wait to go to Disneyworld again!' she said excitedly.

'How many times have you been?' Velvet asked interestedly.

'Twice. But they were ages ago, when I was a baby.'

'Five isn't being a baby,' her father put in dryly.

'No—Tony's a baby.' Her sleep obviously hadn't

made her forget about him. 'Can I see your little boy, Velvet?' she wanted to know.

'I—Well——'

'He's in England, Vicki,' Jerard interrupted her halting reply.

'I know. I meant when we get back. Can I, Velvet?'

Velvet didn't know what to say. She couldn't really see any real reason why Vicki and Tony shouldn't meet. They would probably like each other, both full of mischief. But if Vicki and Tony met then she and Jerard would probably have to meet too, and she didn't want to see him again once she returned home.

He upset her, made her uncertain, both of her past and her future. Until she had met him she had been secure in her love for Anthony, in her marriage, and now he had made her doubt even that. Her secure little world seemed to be fast disappearing.

And there was another reason she didn't want to see him again, a reason that frightened her. She was attracted to him! When he had kissed her yesterday, touched her, she hadn't wanted him to stop. Even now she still tingled from his caressing hands, the feel of his lips on hers, and she was frightened of the emotions he aroused within her. Her body remembered him even if she didn't, and maybe the next time he kissed her she wouldn't be able to call a halt to it. Not that he had since given her the impression that he wanted to kiss her again, the opposite in fact; his disgust with what he called her lies was more than obvious.

'Velvet?' Vicki prompted anxiously.

'I——' she looked at Jerard, but this time he didn't appear to want to help her out. 'I don't see why not, Vicki,' she finally answered. 'I'm sure Tony would love to meet you.'

'Oh, good!' her face glowed.

Velvet's heart softened. What harm could it do to

agree? Vicki might forget all about it by the time she got back to England.

'My daughter never forgets,' Jerard told her softly, obviously guessing her thoughts.

'Then she must be like you,' she snapped back resentfully.

His mouth twisted. 'We don't all have your convenient lapses of memory.'

She paled. 'You think I enjoy having forgotten my own husband.'

'I think you would enjoy having *me* think you had,' he scorned.

'And why would I enjoy that?'

'Then you could be sure that I thought you'd forgotten how good we were together too. God,' he groaned softly, his hands fiercely gripping the steering-wheel, 'I used to wake up in a cold sweat remembering what it was like with you!'

'Please, Jerard—Vicki!' she reminded her tautly.

'My daughter isn't stupid, Velvet,' he rasped. 'She's perfectly well aware of the fact that there's an—awareness between us.'

'No!' she gasped.

'Yes,' he insisted grimly. 'Why do you think she likes to see the two of us together? And believe me, I'm no happier about it than you are.'

His tone was so insulting that Velvet clammed up for the rest of the journey, talking solely to Vicki. Not that it seemed to bother Jerard, he chatted quite easily with both of them, not seeming to care that he received no answers from Velvet.

'I'd forgotten that you sulk,' he said with amusement as Vicki bounded ahead of them into the hotel and the Ferrari was taken to be parked by one of the hotel workers.

She glared up at him. 'I do not sulk!'

'You do,' Jerard grinned, carrying her overnight bag and another suitcase she presumed contained his and Vicki's clothes. 'I vividly remember one occasion when you sulked. I remember even more vividly the method I used to get you out of it.'

By the sensuous curve of his lips, and the warmth in his eyes, it didn't take much to guess that method. 'Do you have to get so damned personal all the time!' she snapped before walking on ahead, catching Vicki up, the two of them waiting at the desk for Jerard to join them, his strides leisurely.

'Mr Daniels!' the manager appeared as if from nowhere, shaking Jerard's hand warmly. 'It's good to see you again. And you've brought your wife and daughter with you this time,' he smiled at Velvet.

'I'm not Mrs Daniels,' she told him quietly, a high colour to her cheeks.

'Oh. Oh, I see.' His smile deepened. 'Well, it's nice to meet you, anyway.'

Velvet looked appealingly at Jerard. The manager had obviously assumed that she was Jerard's live-in girl-friend, and she wanted that impression dispelled as soon as possible.

With a mocking smile in her direction Jerard answered the other man. 'Mrs Dale is a friend of my daughter,' he drawled.

It wasn't exactly the explanation Velvet had been expecting, although it was in fact the true one.

'But Daddy likes her too,' Vicki put in innocently, looking up affectionately at Velvet as she held her hand.

'Out of the mouths of babes . . .' Jerard murmured so that only Velvet should hear him. 'It's been a long drive, Mike,' he told the other man briskly. 'If you'll excuse us?'

'Of course,' the manager nodded. 'Everything has been done to make your stay with us enjoyable, but if there's anything you need . . .'

'We'll ask for it,' Jerard nodded.

'Let me get someone to take up your luggage——'

'It's okay,' Jerard dismissed, 'I can manage.' He strode over to the lift, Vicki and Velvet following behind him. 'Bed for you, young lady,' he told Vicki firmly as they travelled up in the lift.

'Oh, but——'

'Bed!'

Vicki looked rebellious. 'But it's early yet. I thought we could all——'

'*We* aren't doing anything,' she was told as they stepped out of the lift. 'Hot milk for you, bath, and then bed.'

'Can Velvet bath me?' she asked as a compromise.

He raised his dark eyebrows. 'Velvet?'

'I'd love to,' she nodded.

'Okay,' Jerard shrugged. 'But don't blame me if you get soaked, this young lady likes to play games in the bath—like another young lady I know,' he added softly.

Vicki looked up at him. 'What did you say, Daddy?'

'Nothing important.' He put their cases down, ruffling her hair before opening the door.

Velvet's cheeks were fiery red. Jerard's implication was clear; she was the other 'young lady' who liked to play games in the bath—with him? God, what else could he have meant! The idea of it was—exhilarating!

She picked up her small case. 'If you'll tell me where my room is . . .?'

Jerard pushed the door open and went inside. 'Step this way, Mrs Dale,' he mocked. 'And I'll show it to you.'

Her eyes widened. 'I—I can't stay in there with you!'

'Why not?' his eyes were narrowed. 'It is a suite, after all. With four bedrooms,' he added tauntingly.

'Yes, but I——' her hand tightened on the handle of

her case. 'I'd rather have a room of my own.'

'We can talk this out later,' he looked pointedly at the listening Vicki. 'Come inside for now.'

She went reluctantly. She couldn't possibly stay the night here, even if it was a suite.

Jerard was right, she did get soaked helping Vicki with her bath, but she had a lot of fun too. Without her clothes Vicki was painfully thin, her hair secured on top of her head to keep it dry making her look even more so. And yet she was a robust child, with a healthy glow to her cheeks.

It felt strange to be bathing a child of this size; she was only used to the tiny squirming bundle that Tony usually was. But Vicki looked angelic with her face newly washed and shiny, her hair glossily clean, her pink cotton nightgown reaching down to her ankles.

She came out to the lounge to drink the warm milk her father had ordered for her, accepting demurely when he ordered her to bed once she had drunk it, evidence that she was tired, even though she wasn't going to admit it.

'I want you both to take me to bed,' she requested shyly.

Jerard looked at Velvet. 'All right,' he agreed as he saw her nod. 'Just this once.'

Vicki went quite happily into the bedroom, a hand in each of theirs, and climbed beneath the bedclothes. 'Now you both have to tuck me in,' she announced mischievously.

'Vicki——'

'Oh, please, Daddy,' she pleaded. 'Just for tonight!'

He shrugged. 'Okay,' he agreed indulgently.

'Right. You sit here,' she ordered him to sit on one side of the bed, 'and you here,' she ordered Velvet to the other side. 'Now I want you both to kiss me good-night.'

'You seem to have a lot of "I wants" tonight,' her father said sternly.

'Daddy!'

He bent to kiss her on the forehead. 'You're very bossy tonight, young lady.'

'I know,' she grinned. 'But it's so nice having you both here, it's almost like——'

'Vicki, no!' He moved back, standing up. 'Behave yourself!'

'But I was only going to say it's almost like having a mummy and a daddy.' Her arms came up lovingly about Velvet's neck. 'I was thinking——'

'When you start thinking it usually means trouble,' her father said grimly.

She looked appealingly at Velvet. 'It's just that your little boy doesn't have a daddy, and I don't have a mummy, and I wondered——'

'Vicki, for God's sake!' her father exploded.

Her mouth set rebelliously, her arms tightening about Velvet's neck. 'Will you be my mummy, Velvet?' she asked shyly.

CHAPTER FIVE

VELVET didn't know what to do, what to say. The question had been so unexpected that she was just speechless. Looked at from Vicki's point of view it would seem a perfectly natural request, even a logical one, so much so that Velvet didn't have an answer to it.

'It's time you were asleep, Vicki,' Jerard said briskly.

She pouted. 'But Velvet hasn't answered me.'

'And she isn't going to,' he told her firmly. 'I've warned you once today about asking questions like this, I'm not going to tell you again.' He tucked the covers about her. 'Now get to sleep,' he switched off the main light, leaving the night-lamp on. 'It's going to be a long exciting day tomorrow.' He took hold of Velvet's arm and led her over to the door. ''Night, darling,' he said huskily to his daughter.

''Night, Daddy,' she yawned. 'Velvet, you—you aren't cross with me, are you?' she asked uncertainly.

Velvet came out of her stupor. 'No, of course I'm not, Vicki,' she said with forced brightness.

'Good. Because I like you very, very much.' She closed her eyes sleepily.

'Hell!' Jerard swore as soon as they were in the lounge and Vicki's bedroom door was firmly closed. 'Hell and damnation!' He paced the room angrily.

Velvet pushed her tousled hair back from her face. 'I heard you the first time,' she said shakily.

He turned on her fiercely. 'I warned you about this. I——'

'Yes, you warned me!' she snapped. 'How like you to turn around and say "I told you so"!'

88

'How would you know it was like me?' his mouth twisted. 'When you say you don't even know me?'

'I——'

'I'll tell you how well you know me,' his fingers dug into her shoulders as he shook her. 'You know me so well that you only used to say one word and I'd be in bed with you.'

'Jerard——'

'That's the word!' he said grimly, his mouth coming down forcefully on hers.

She hadn't wanted him to kiss her, had been afraid that he would. She melted against him at the first touch of his lips, her body arching against the hard contours of his, her fingers entangled in the dark thickness of his hair.

Lips met lips, exploringly, Jerard's body hardening against her, his hands moving feverishly across her back. He swung her up in his arms and carried her over to the sofa, his mouth not leaving hers as he lay down beside her, his lips continuing their exploration.

Jerard was the one to finally break the kiss, his eyes dark as he looked down at her, his breathing ragged. 'Are you sure this is what you want, Velvet? he asked huskily.

'Oh yes,' her hands clung about his throat, 'this is what I want.' It was what her body cried out for, what she hungered for.

She had been too long denied this male warmth, the feel and smell of Jerard invading her senses, making her head spin. She pressed herself against him, instantly feeling the surge of passion in his body.

'And God knows I want you,' he groaned, his tongue tracing the outline of her lips, daring further intimacies as they parted to that sensual caress. 'God, Velvet!' His mouth once more claimed hers, moving hungrily against her.

So much for her assertion that this would never

happen again! But she didn't care. As long as Jerard went on touching her, kissing her, she didn't care about anything else. Not even her baby waiting at home for her in England mattered at this moment.

She offered no resistance as Jerard pushed up the tee-shirt she had worn for travelling; in fact she helped him, slipping her arms out of her bra-straps as he unfastened the clasp. She gasped as his mouth claimed one aroused nipple, his teeth biting erotically, shooting waves of pleasure through her body, from the tips of her toes to her tingling scalp.

That feeling of familiarity washed over her once again, and she acted instinctively, unbuttoning his shirt, her hands going to his back, her nails digging into his skin.

His breath caught in his throat. 'I always liked that,' he moaned. 'Let's see what else you can remember that I like.'

She was a willing pupil to his teaching, and their caresses became even more intimate as she helped Jerard remove his shirt, her own tee-shirt soon joining the silky material on the carpeted floor, their torsos searing together in heated passion.

The tips of her breasts ached from contact with Jerard's hair-roughened chest, their legs were entwined as they moved together for even closer contact. Velvet knew that the two of them were going to make love fully, knew it and craved for it.

But the sudden knock on the door took that final commitment out of their hands, and Jerard broke away from her reluctantly.

'God, no!' he groaned, his face in her throat.

'Who can it be?' she whispered.

'Dinner,' he said ruefully, standing up to pull on his shirt.

'Dinner . . .?' she grimaced.

'Mm,' he picked up her bra and tee-shirt, handing

them to her. 'I ordered it while you were bathing Vicki. I wish now that I hadn't bothered.' His eyes still blazed with desire.

Velvet sat up, hastily pulling on her clothes as the knock was repeated. 'I—I didn't realise.'

Reaction was starting to set in, embarrassment, but not shame, washing over her. She had no reason to feel shame, and she didn't. As Carly had already pointed out, she was free, over twenty-one, and perfectly capable of deciding whether or not she wanted to go to bed with a man. And she did want to go to bed with Jerard.

'Later, Velvet,' he correctly read the hunger in her eyes. 'I don't welcome this interruption any more than you do,' his thumb caressed the pulsing swell of her bottom lip. 'Later,' he repeated huskily, his word a promise.

Her breathing was shallow, she was still deeply affected by what had just happened between them. 'I—I'm presentable now,' she told him softly, pulling the tee-shirt down over her lacy-covered breasts.

'You're always presentable, Velvet,' he murmured throatily. 'But when you're naked, then you're—breathtaking.'

She flushed. 'The door,' she reminded him, his reference to her nakedness only seeming to remind her of all she couldn't remember. Oh, how she wished she could remember loving and being loved by this man, it must have been the most fantastic experience of her life.

No! Loving and being loved by Anthony had been that! She paled as she remembered her husband, the man she had loved since she was nineteen.

'Velvet?' Jerard queried sharply.

She looked up at him dazedly, frowning. 'Yes?' Her voice was hesitant, bewildered.

'I—Oh damn!' he swore as the knock sounded again, walking over angrily to answer it.

It was indeed their dinner, and Velvet had time to regain her composure while the waiter set it out on the dining-room table. She wasn't free at all, she had a husband and son she owed her loyalty to. She might feel like making love with Jerard, but she couldn't do it, couldn't betray Anthony's memory in that way, or his son that she was bringing up so lovingly.

'It's gone, isn't it?' Jerard said once they were alone, the waiter having silently left.

She blinked hard. 'I'm sorry?' she shook her head in puzzlement. 'What's gone?'

He shrugged resignedly. 'The moment—it's gone.'

She bit her lip. 'I——'

'Don't bother to explain, Velvet,' his voice was harsh. 'Come and eat your food,' he ordered curtly.

She looked at him pleadingly. 'Jerard——'

'Eat!'

'I'm not hungry,' she muttered. 'It isn't long since I last ate.'

'It's over four hours ago, and as I remember you didn't eat at all. You'll eat now.' He attacked his steak as if it had done him some personal harm.

She sat down, picking up her knife and fork. She even managed to raise a piece of steak to her lips, but she couldn't quite bring herself to put it in her mouth. 'I can't!' Her fork landed back on her plate with a clatter. 'I just can't!' She pushed back her chair and ran into the bedroom Jerard had put her case into earlier, shutting the door behind her to lean weakly back against it.

She was pushed forward as the door jerked open, would have fallen if Jerard's arm hadn't come about her waist, pulling her back against him, his face in her hair.

'I'm not going to force you.' His breath ruffled her red-gold hair. Velvet licked her dry lips. 'I—I didn't think you would.'

'Didn't you?' He sounded amused.

'No,' she shook her head.

'Come back and eat your food.' He spun her gently round, his hands on her arms. 'Come on,' his tone was gentle too. 'When we've eaten we can listen to some music, relax a little.'

'I——'

'I need you, Velvet.'

She swallowed hard, seeming to stop breathing altogether. 'You—you need me?' Again she licked her lips, stopping as she realised by the darkening of his eyes how provocative he found the unconscious movement.

Jerard drew a ragged, controlling breath. 'Last night I had very little sleep, today I've driven for over four hours. Right now I need to be with someone I can relax with.'

'And you—you can relax with me?' She couldn't relax with him at all, feeling as taut as a bowstring.

Jerard gave a rueful smile. 'I can try. I don't want to be alone, Velvet,' he added seriously. 'I just need—company, your company.'

'All right,' she agreed softly. 'But I really don't think I can eat.'

'Then just have some wine. It will help you relax.'

It was a nice wine, white and bubbly, a little like champagne. Jerard didn't do full justice to the meal either, although he asked the waiter to leave the wine as he cleared the other debris of the meal away.

'Now for the music,' Jerard said once they were alone again, moving to the stereo and vast supply of records in the adjoining cabinet. 'What do you suggest?'

'Johnny Mathis?'

'Mm, I think there are a couple of his.' He flicked through the collection, taking one out of the rack. 'I seem to remember you used to like Rod Stewart.'

She smiled. 'I still do.'

Jerard grimaced. 'But not to make love to. I remember finding it very *un*sexy listening to Rod Stewart sing 'If you think I'm sexy' when I was trying to make love to you.'

Her mouth quirked with humour. 'What happened?'

He shrugged. 'We landed up in hysterics.'

'I'm not surprised!' She was starting to feel less embarrassed about his revelations from the past, although that was probably due to the wine she had consumed.

He put the Johnny Mathis record on the turntable. 'This is much more romantic.'

Panic washed over her. 'Perhaps I ought to go to bed now.' She put down her wine glass. 'I—I never did get anything done about a seperate room,' she said nervously.

'There's really no need. There are more than enough rooms here. I've said I won't force you, Velvet, and I won't.' His eyes were compelling. 'It isn't my way at all.'

'I don't suppose it's ever needed to be,' she choked. His eyes narrowed. 'If you're trying to find out if I forced you before then the answer is no,' he rasped. 'We met quite accidentally on the beach one day, fell in love, and after that there was no question of not spending every moment of that week together, day and night.'

'But what was I doing in Florida?'

'The same as you are this time, working. You were working for me then, too.'

'And that's how I was able to take the week off,' she derided.

'Yes,' he snapped tautly, moving towards her. 'Is that what it was, Velvet? A case of sleeping with the boss and seeing what you could get out of it?'

She stood up, suddenly pale. 'I think I'll go to my room now. And just for the record, Mr Daniels, did I ever ask you for anything?'

'No, I *offered* it. I offered you marriage,' he revealed bitterly.

'And I married Anthony.' Her mouth twisted. 'So much for that theory, Mr Daniels. Perhaps you can give it a little more thought and come up with the answer as to why I married Anthony, if it isn't already obvious enough.'

'You loved him!' Jerard rasped.

'That's right,' she nodded coolly. 'And whatever time I spent with you was just an impetuous interlude—and one I would rather forget had ever happened.'

'I thought you already had,' he scorned.

Her head was held high. 'I have, but *you* haven't.'

'And I don't ever intend to. It will serve to remind me of the deceit of women, something I'd forgotten by loving you.' He turned his back on her.

Velvet went to her room, the temporary truce between them definitely over, although for Vicki's sake she had to try and act as if there were no friction between Jerard and herself. Friction! It was such intense sexual awareness she could feel it even now, could sense his presence on the other side of her bedroom wall, his room being the one next to hers.

She found it hard to sleep, although she didn't fear Jerard's intrusion at all. He had said he wouldn't force her, and she knew he wouldn't. She knew that much about him at least.

She was slowly learning more and more about two years ago, had learnt that she must have thought herself very much in love with Jerard, that he had deeply returned that love, that he had been separated from his wife but that she was still engaged to Anthony.

She must have thought herself very much in love with Jerard to have betrayed Anthony in that way, and according to Jerard she had even agreed to marry him, something that had never become fact—because of his family commitments, Jerard said.

She didn't even know she had been in Florida before, but Simon must know about it, so perhaps he could shed some light on it; he might even know about Jerard! Her brother had never mentioned another man when she had asked him about that blank eleven months, but then he probably wouldn't know the whole story, and what he did know perhaps hadn't seemed important as she had later married Anthony.

Nevertheless, she had to find out what he did know. She could hardly contain her curiosity until she got home. Home. Tomorrow she would be back in England, would take Tony back to the flat they shared, and then maybe she could forget all about meeting Jerard Daniels—for the second time.

After the way they had parted the evening before Velvet was perfectly prepared to put up with Jerard's angry mockery; instead he was charming, laughing and joking with both Vicki and herself as they breakfasted together.

'Can I go in Tunnel Mountain this time, Daddy?' Vicki asked excitedly. 'You said I was too small last time.'

'You haven't grown much,' he teased, perfectly relaxed, looking handsome in a dark green shirt and black trousers, his tanned hair-roughened chest revealed by the open neck of his shirt.

It was a beautiful day outside, the sun was shining brightly, and the weather seemed to reflect their mood.

'I've grown a lot,' Vicki said indignantly.

'I hadn't noticed,' he taunted dryly.

'That's because——' Vicki broke off, biting ier lip.

Jerard's expression sharpened. 'Because what, Vicki?' he prompted softly.

'Nothing,' she mumbled.

'Vicki,' he persisted gently.

'Because—because you went away,' the little girl choked. 'You went away and left me,' she added in a quavery voice.

Velvet looked sympathetically at Jerard's pale face, as she stood up. 'I think I'll just go and get my handbag,' she said brightly, leaving father and daughter alone.

Vicki was a highly sensitive little girl, and if her parents had separated, as Jerard had said they had, then her feelings of rejection were perfectly understandable. Broken marriages were always harder on the children.

A knock sounded on Velvet's bedroom door several minutes later, and Jerard entered without waiting for acknowledgement of that knock. He looked like a man who had just been on the receiving end of a painful blow.

'Are you all right?' Velvet asked concernedly.

His expression was bleak. 'My daughter has just informed me that I don't really love her.'

'Oh no!'

'Yes,' he said heavily, sitting down on the bed.

It had obviously shaken him, and Velvet's heart went out to him. 'But why should she think such a thing?'

'My wife,' he revealed harshly. 'When Tina and I first parted it wasn't an amicable separation, far from it, in fact. Tina was very bitter, and I didn't realise until it was too late that she had passed that bitterness on to Vicki. Tina told her that I didn't love or want her any more.'

'That's cruel!' Velvet shook her head with the cruelty of it.

He shrugged. 'It's human nature, I suppose. When you're hurt you hit out at the nearest person—and Vicki was the closest as far as Tina was concerned.'

Velvet frowned. 'But she must realise now that you love her?'

He sighed. 'I think she does, until something like this

blows up.' He stood up· 'We should be going, Vicki is waiting for us.'

There was still the trace of tears on Vicki's cheeks, but otherwise her outburst might never have taken place. Jerard acted as if it hadn't either, continuing to tease his daughter as they went to collect the car, giving Vicki some money to go and get some sweets from the hotel shop.

'You're puzzled, aren't you?' he said to Velvet.

'A little,' she nodded.

'That's understandable. But I've been assured by experts, a number of them, that it's better to ignore these moods of Vicki's. They tell me that if I just continue to show her I love her she'll grow out of them.'

Velvet's eyes widened. 'Vicki is seeing a psychiatrist?'

He gave the ghost of a smile. 'Nothing that serious. She was very disturbed by her mother's death—a lot of children are. You'll probably have some problems of your own once your son is old enough to ask questions.' His voice had hardened perceptibly as he spoke of Tony. 'Once I've made Vicki secure in my love, something that's a lot harder to do than you think, she should stop having these bouts of near-hysteria.'

Remembering the times she had seen them, and the rapidity with which the moods passed, Velvet thought he was probably making good progress. The crying in the night had been the worst time, but even that had passed quite quickly.

'Don't concern yourself, Velvet,' Jerard gave a strained smile. 'This is my problem.'

'Yes, but——'

'I'll work it out,' he told her firmly. 'Now let's make an effort to enjoy this day out together that's been forced on us.'

She flinched as if he had hit her, and was glad that Vicki chose that moment to rejoin them. Jerard was making it obvious that although he was being outwardly pleasant he would rather she was anywhere else but here with him.

But his act was a convincing one, so much so that she felt able to relax with him on the drive to Disneyworld. Vicki sat by the window as they took the monorail from the car park into Disneyworld itself, Velvet pressed up against Jerard's other side, their bodies meeting from thigh to knee. It was impossible to move away, as another man was sitting on her other side, although he in no way affected her like Jerard did; the whole of that side of her body seemed to tingle.

The car had been left in Pluto car park—all the car parks were named after Disney characters. From the car park they had taken an open bus to the pay desks, and from there they had chose to be transported into Disneyworld by the monorail instead of the paddle-steamer. The monorail went straight through the middle of a hotel, through the dining-room in fact, something Vicki found highly amusing. It was rather strange to be going through a room that contained people eating a meal, although the diners seemed to take the appearance of the monorail for granted.

'Before you ask, the answer is no,' Jerard told Vicki firmly.

She looked disappointed. 'Oh, but——'

'No, Vicki. We wouldn't have time for anything else if we ate there.'

Velvet had to admire the way he was indulgently firm with Vicki. A lot of men in his position would be inclined to spoil the little girl, but not Jerard. He let her know she was loved, but he did it with a quiet discipline Vicki couldn't help but respect. Velvet had no doubt he would win through in the end.

Entering Disneyworld was like entering the world of her childhood dreams—old-fashioned trams and horse-

drawn buggies, an old-fashioned bus driving people up
and down Main Street. As they walked along the spot-
lessly clean sidewalk they passed a gift shop, an old
cinema, an old-fashioned ice-cream parlour, and a
flower market. Once they reached the end of Main Street
they came to a replica of the Crystal Palace, and directly
in front of them, dominating the skyline, was the fairytale castle.

'I'd forgotten,' Jerard murmured at her side.

She blinked up at him. 'Forgotten what?'

'The magic of this place.' He smiled a completely
genuine smile. 'You should see your face,' he explained.
'You're spellbound. At this moment you don't look any
older than Vicki.'

She blushed, at once feeling foolish. 'I'm sorry.
I——'

'No, don't apologise,' he cut in forcefully. 'And don't
lose that look. Come on,' he took hold of her hand, 'I'll
buy you some popcorn.'

It was indeed a magic place, for grown-ups as well as
children, a world of makebelieve that you became completely caught up in. The rides were spectacular, although Velvet cried off Tunnel Mountain after seeing
the warning outside for young children and nervous
people. Not that she was either of those things, but she
had invariably got sick on such rides as a child, and
Vicki came back looking a bit green.

They went on everything, from Futureworld to
Adventureland, but the Pirates of the Caribbean was
Velvet's favourite, the mechanical people so well
animated they looked real. They watched the parade of
Disney characters in the afternoon too—all the old
favourites, Donald Duck, Mickey Mouse, and most of
the Jungle Book characters.

The Haunted House was good too. Jerard bought
them an early dinner in a tavern close by, the girls in

here dressed up as serving wenches, the decor strictly in keeping with the era.

'We'll have to be leaving soon,' he said once they emerged out into the evening sunshine.

'Oh, not yet, Daddy!' Vicki's face dropped with disappointment. 'I wanted to see the castle all lighted—alight——'

'Lit up,' her father provided. 'And that won't be happening for a couple of hours yet.' It was still quite light.

'I'm sure Velvet would like to see the lights too, Daddy,' she told him, her blue eyes, so like his own, widely innocent.

'I think that you might border on blackmail, Vicki,' Velvet chided.

'Would you like to see the lights?' Jerard queried tolerantly.

'Well . . . yes.' She looked at him hopefully. He had been so patient up to now, had done everything Vicki suggested, but he still had that long drive back to Fort Lauderdale. 'But it's your decision,' she added reasonably.

'We'll stay.'

'Oh, good!' Vicki threw her arms about his throat. 'Can I go on It's a Small World again?' she asked excitedly.

He nodded. 'Velvet and I will wait for you over here,' he indicated some seats a short distance away. 'I think twice is enough for us. We'll see you later.' He took the Mickey Mouse from her that Velvet had bought her earlier in the day, the stuffed toy leaving her for the first sime since its purchase. It had even had to sit up at the table with them while they ate!

'Don't lose him,' Vicki warned.

'I won't,' her father promised before she disappeared into the crowd.

'Phew!' Velvet sank down gratefully on to the seat. 'I'm exhausted!'

Jerard still looked as fresh as when they had set out that morning, although they must literally have walked miles during the last few hours. 'I thought you might be,' he smiled. 'Which is why I told Vicki to go off on her own. I for one have seen enough of It's a Small World,' he grimaced, sitting down beside her.

So had she, but it had been very good—small mobile dolls dressed up in national dresses from all over the world, seen from a boat ride that took you through each changing scene. 'She's enjoying herself.'

He quirked a teasing eyebrow at her. 'So are you.'

She gave a happy laugh. 'I think we're all children at heart.'

'You certainly are.' His arm rested lightly along her shoulders. 'I've enjoyed today, and mainly because you made it enjoyable. I have to admit I wasn't really looking forward to coming here, but you've helped take the strain out of it. Vicki can be a little—difficult at times.'

'She likes your undivided attention. Tony went—I'm sorry,' she bit her lip awkwardly.

'Tony went . . .?' he prompted.

She looked down at her hands. 'He went through a stage like that a couple of months ago. I believe it happens a lot with single-parent families.'

'Probably,' he agreed seriously. 'Maybe I should get married again.'

'Yes—yes, perhaps you should.' She moved away from him, finding the idea of him marrying anyone slightly sickening. She found she had become vaguely possessive over Vicki too, liking the way the little girl ran to her and threw her arms impetuously about her.

This wouldn't do! She had her own child to go back to, her own life to lead. And it didn't include this man!

'How about you?' Jerard queried casually. 'Is there a man in your life?'

Only him! 'Not at the moment,' she invaded. 'You?'

'The same,' he shrugged.

'I——'

'Hey, Daddy,' Vicki appeared in front of them, breaking the moment of intimacy as she jumped up and down. 'The lights are going on!' She took hold of their hands and pulled them both to their feet. 'Let's go and look.'

If anything everywhere looked even more beautiful now that it was dark and the lights had come on, even more like a fairytale, and it was with great reluctance that they finally left an hour later. Vicki fell asleep in the back of the car soon after they got away from Disneyworld.

'Maybe we should stay at the hotel another night,' Velvet suggested tentatively. 'After all, you must be tired too.' She looked questioningly at Jerard.

'I don't think that would be a good idea,' he said deeply.

'Why?' she frowned. 'We could drive back in the morning, my plane doesn't leave until the afternoon.'

'It just isn't a good idea,' he repeated grimly. 'Vicki's already asleep, once we get on the straight road you can join her.'

'But——'

'We're going back to Fort Lauderdale tonight,' he rasped. 'I don't want you to miss your plane.'

He couldn't have told her more clearly that he was now anxious to get rid of her. He hadn't wanted her along on this trip in the first place, and even though he was grateful for her help with Vicki, he now wanted her out of his life as soon as possible.

It was a blow to her, his urgency to be parted from her, her own attraction towards him having deepened throughout the day. She had been beginning to think it wouldn't be such a bad idea for Vicki and Tony to meet, then she would be able to see Jerard again. But he didn't share her desire for further meetings between them—that much was proved to her later that evening as they parted for the night after the long journey, Vicki held securely in Jerard's arms, still fast asleep.

'Thank you for today,' Velvet said softly so as not to disturb the sleeping child.

'That's okay,' he said tersely. 'Thank *you*.'

'Oh, I didn't do anything.'

'You were there. Vicki appreciated it.'

She swallowed hard, strangely reluctant to part from him. 'Do I owe you anything—for my food—and things?'

'No,' he rasped. 'Get to bed now, Velvet. It's late.'

He didn't even say goodbye to her the next day. She didn't see anything of either him or Vicki. When she enquired at the desk she was told that Mr and Miss Daniels were both out, and that they didn't know when to expect them back.

'No goodbye?'

She spun round to find Greg standing behind her, and was hardly able to contain her disappointment. She had hoped it was Jerard, as Paul, Carly and herself were just booking out of the hotel. And still there was no sign of Jerard or Vicki!

She gave a bright smile. 'I would have found you before I left.'

'But you're just going,' he said accusingly.

'Just checking out,' she corrected. 'We don't leave for a few minutes yet.'

He pulled her to one side. 'I wish you'd told me about you and Mr Daniels,' he said reproachfully. 'I could have really put my foot in it with him.'

Velvet frowned. 'I don't see how.'

'Well—You and he——'

'Now wait a minute,' she interrupted firmly. 'He and I, what?'

Greg looked uncomfortable. 'I was talking to one of the other employees, and he remembers you and Mr Daniels being here together before.'

She went very pale, swallowing hard. 'He does?' Was that croaky voice really hers?

'Mm,' Greg nodded. 'A couple of years back. And he says the two of you were really close even then.'

'I see.' She bit her lip. So it really was true, she really had spent that time here with Jerard! 'Do we look "close" now?' She looked at Greg unflinchingly.

'Not that I've seen. But you have just been away with him!'

'I went to be with his daughter, not him.'

Greg looked sceptical. 'If you say so—not that it's any of my business anyway.' He grinned. 'You've been longing to say that, haven't you?'

She laughed up at him. 'How did you guess?'

'It wasn't hard.' He bent to kiss her lightly on the mouth. 'Take care, Velvet.'

'You too, Greg.'

'I hate to break up this touching little scene,' cut in a mocking voice, 'but don't you have a plane to catch, Mrs Dale?'

Jerard! And he was calling her 'Mrs Dale' again. He was alone, looking formally attractive in a lightweight cream suit and contrasting brown shirt. Velvet's heart skipped a beat as she looked at him, his sensuality reaching out and captivating her.

'See you,' Greg said softly before disappearing back into his office.

'Ready?' Paul and Carly joined herself and Jerard.

'I—Yes, I'm ready. Goodbye, Mr Daniels——'

'Not goodbye, Velvet,' he said mockingly. 'I'm driving

you to the airport, didn't you know that?'

'No,' she mumbled. All that worry that she wasn't going to see him again before she left and all the time he had been going to drive them to Miami! 'Paul didn't tell me,' she added accusingly.

'I've hardly seen you lately to tell you anything,' Paul told her pointedly.

Paul and Carly got into the back of the car, so Velvet of necessity had to sit in the front beside Jerard. 'Where's Vicki this afternoon?' she asked him.

'With Faye,' he revealed abruptly. 'She has no idea you're leaving today.'

'Oh.'

'Oh indeed,' he drawled grimly. 'She thinks I'm at a business meeting.'

Velvet frowned. 'Is that wise?.

'Of course it isn't wise!' he snapped. 'But I didn't feel up to the scene this morning. She was pleased to have Faye back, but only because she thought she would be seeing you later. Still, it isn't your problem, is it?'

Another slap in the face for her. She had to bite her tongue to stop herself from giving him a sharp retort, but was conscious of Paul and Carly. Instead she chose to remain silent, and the journey to Miami passed with Jerard and Paul discussing business.

Velvet hadn't envisaged Jerard seeing them off at the airport, and a curious lump rose in her throat as it came time to say goodbye. He shook hands with Paul and Carly first.

Velvet licked her lips nervously as he turned to her, unsure what to say—or do. Jerard had no such reservations.

'Goodbye, Mrs Dale,' he held out his hand to her as formally as he had to the other couple. 'Thank you for taking care of my daughter the last couple of days. I appreciate it.'

Not enough to drop the formality, obviously. 'I enjoyed it,' she said stiffly. 'Goodbye, Mr Daniels,' she added as their flight was called.

'Goodbye,' he nodded tersely, his expression remote.

Her chin went up, her head held high as she walked with Paul and Carly to the departure gate. She handed her boarding card over, finally plucking up the courage to turn. He had already gone—Jerard had gone!.

'It didn't work out, hmm?' Carly said gently.

'There was nothing *to* work out,' Velvet replied abruptly.

'But——'

'Please, Carly, I'd rather not talk about it just now. I—I have a headache.'

She did indeed have a headache as she tried to hold back the tears for most of the nine-hour flight, each minute taking her closer to Tony—but farther away from Jerard!

CHAPTER SIX

IN typical English summer fashion it was raining when they arrived back at Heathrow in the early hours of the morning, made all the more miserable for Velvet because she had told Simon not to meet her, that she would spend what was left of the night at her apartment and pick Tony up in the morning.

Paul and Carly dropped her off from their taxi on the way to their own flat, arranging to meet on Monday to finish off the photographs.

There was about Velvet a deep air of depression, and she was almost afraid to delve into the reason behind it. But she couldn't help it, unable to sleep even though she was exhausted by the flight, and the bed looked very inviting.

But Jerard Daniels wouldn't be banished from her mind, tall and handsome as she had seen him last, his commanding appearance demanding and receiving respect. He had been nothing like the man she had met that first day, the half demented man who had claimed to be in love with her.

And yet now she loved him! She acknowledged it even as she wondered how it could have happened, when it had happened. But this yearning ache inside her to be back at his side told her that it was a fact. She was in love with a man she didn't even know, a man she might never see again.

But maybe she would, maybe Vicki would make him keep his promise to let her come and meet Tony, and maybe he would be the one to bring her. That was an awful lot of maybes—but at the moment that was all she had.

She almost fainted with shock when the telephone began ringing. Who on earth could be telephoning this time of morning? Unless it was Simon checking to see if she had arrived home all right—it would be just like him, he had always been a protective brother.

'Simon——'

'Velvet,' interrupted a deeply impatient voice—Jerard's voice!

'Velvet!' Vicki's childish tones cut in excitedly. 'Velvet, is that you?'

'Why, yes. But——'

'We're coming home, Velvet,' the little girl cut in. 'Can I still come and see you?'

'Well, yes. But——'

'That's enough, Vicki,' Jerard could be heard saying firmly. 'Off to bed, I'll handle it from here. Bed, Vicki,' he repeated as he obviously received further argument. 'Velvet?' he came back on the line, so disturbing when she had been thinking about him so intently.

'Jerard . . .' she breathed huskily.

For long timeless seconds there was silence on the other end of the line. 'Are you feeling well?' he asked finally.

'Yes, fine.' Just a bit overawed, especially after so recently discovering she loved him. 'Don't I sound fine?' she asked brightly.

'No. Did I wake you, is that it?'

'I said I was all right,' she insisted sharply.

'You sound—strange.'

'Maybe I am,' she flared angrily, feeling frustrated with the stupidity of this conversation. 'Or maybe I'm just tired,' she snapped. 'Goodnight, Mr Daniels!' She slammed the telephone receiver back on its cradle.

How could Jerard call her just to insult her! Tears

were streaming down her face when the telephone began ringing again. She let it ring and ring, shutting herself in her bedroom to shut out its noise. It finally stopped, only to start up again a few seconds later. This time when it stopped she quickly removed it from its cradle, making sure Jerard couldn't reach her again.

It sounded as if Vicki were being difficult about her departure. But if Jerard had somehow obtained her telephone number then it also followed that he had her address. If Vicki wanted to see her then Jerard would arrange that she did.

Her own behaviour was harder to analyse. She had wanted to talk to Jerard, but not to that cold, mocking stranger, to the warm vibrant man he could be on occasion. How much nicer it would be if all differences could be forgotten between them and they could start again.

But that couldn't happen; Jerard's distrust of her and her own fear of her love for him, both in the past and now, precluded that happening.

She finally put the receiver back about seven o'clock, just in case her brother should want to call her. His call came through about ten minutes later.

'I've been calling for the last half an hour,' he complained. 'It's been engaged the whole time.'

'Welcome home, Velvet,' she taunted sarcastically. 'Did you have a good trip? Yes, it was quite good,' she answered herself. 'But it's nice to be back.'

'Okay,' Simon sighed. 'It is nice to have you back, and did you have a good trip?'

'Not bad.' Then her mood softened, lack of sleep making her brittle when she didn't mean to be. 'How's Tony?'

'Still asleep. But not for long, if I know him.'

'No,' she laughed 'He likes to get up bright and early.'

'So I noticed,' he gave an exaggerated yawn. 'Are you coming over for breakfast?'

'I'd love to,' she accepted eagerly.

'Then hurry up, or your son will have eaten it all.'

'His appetite is still good, hmm?'

'He eats more than I do,' Simon groaned.

Her reunion with her son was a tearful one, on her part. Tony was all beaming smiles, jumping up and down with the excitement of having her back.

She knew she had to talk to Simon about meeting Jerard, and yet she put it off for as long as possible, waiting until Tony went up for his mid-morning nap before broaching the subject.

As it was a Saturday Simon wasn't working, but Janice went out to get the weekend shopping, inviting Velvet to stay over. She accepted, knowing it would give Tony time to adjust before she took him home. Not that he had forgotten her at all, but it wasn't fair to tear him away from the people who had been his family for the last week.

'Okay,' Simon studied her hard, 'let's have it.'

This direct approach instantly disconcerted her. 'Let's have what?' she hedged.

'After a week in Florida, albeit a week of working, you should be glowing with health and vitality, instead of which you look like the "before" part of the health drink advert.'

'Thanks!'

'No, I mean it, Velvet.' He sat forward, his expression serious. 'Did something happen in Florida?'

She bit her lip. 'Not something, some*one*.'

His expression brightened. 'You fell in love?'

'Yes. No! It isn't as simple as that.'

'It never is,' he said dryly.

'There was this man——'

'I already gathered that!'

'I'm serious, Simon,' she said impatiently. 'This man claimed we'd met before——'

'Oh, that one,' he nodded.

'Of course, I told you about him. Well, it seems I did meet him before, only it was during that time I can't remember.'

Simon frowned. 'Then how do you know it's the truth?'

'I just know it, I know *him*. He—I—Did I ever mention anyone called Jerard Daniels to you?'

He shook his head. 'I don't think so.'

'Damn,' she sighed. 'I was hoping you might be able to tell me more about it.'

'Maybe I can,' he said slowly, guardedly. 'You didn't mention any names, but I know there was a man. Maybe it's the same one.'

'It has to be. What did I tell you about him?'

'Nothing. But we guessed he meant something to you.'

'We?' she looked stricken. 'Did Anthony know about Jerard too?'

'Oh yes,' Simon nodded.

And yet he still married me!'

'He loved you.'

'And I let him down!'

'It didn't matter,' her brother shrugged. 'Not to Anthony. He loved you, anyway.'

Velvet drew in a ragged breath. 'But you're quite sure I didn't actually tell you it was Jerard Daniels?'

'Quite sure. I never forget names, you know that.'

'Yes,' she sighed heavily. She wasn't really any further forward, except to know that there definitely had been another man in her life besides Anthony, but then she had already known that, the reaction of her body to Jerard told her that much at least.

Simon was still watching her closely. 'I got the impression this other man was married,' he probed gently.

'He was,' Velvet nodded. 'His wife is dead now.'

Her brother pursed his lips. 'So he's a widower now?'

'Yes.'

'And you're a widow.'

Her mouth quirked with bitter humour. 'And we didn't instantly fall in love with each other again, if that's what you're thinking.' It had taken her about three days to fall in love with Jerard, and about the same amount of time for him to fall *out* of love with her.

'I didn't think you had,' Simon scorned. 'But you obviously felt enough for him for it to have upset you— meeting him again, I mean.'

'I—It—it disturbed me,' she admitted. 'Although I probably wouldn't have seen him again after the first couple of times if it hadn't been for his daughter.' She explained about Vicki's extreme sensitivity.

'I can see you liked her,' Simon smiled.

'Very much,' she confirmed.

Tony woke up at that moment, gabbling away at the top of his voice from the bedroom.

Simon laughed. 'I've never known a child who talks so much and makes absolutely no sense!'

'He says "Mum" quite clearly,' Velvet defended indignantly.

'Big deal!' her brother teased.

Velvet stood up, 'Don't mock until you have children of your own,' she said haughtily, head held high.

He grinned. 'Janice and I are still working on it.'

'After six years you should be about perfect by now.'

Simon laughed. 'We're getting there.'

The weekend passed with lighthearted enjoyment. Janice was possibly the best friend Velvet had ever had as well as being her sister-in-law. They had become firm friends from the moment Simon had brought Janice home to meet the family, and that friendship had been cemented during the time Velvet had lived with Simon and Janice.

Nevertheless, she was glad to leave late on Sunday afternoon, anxious to get back to the normality of the life she led with Tony.

He talked non-stop all the way home, strapped into his baby-seat in the back of the car while she drove. She answered him as if he were making sense, although what he was saying was anyone's guess. One day he would make perfect sense, and until he did he was still a lot of company.

'Choc-choc,' he chortled as they stepped out of the lift, insisting on walking, a newly acquired ability that he insisted on practising every opportunity he could.

'All right,' she laughed. 'I know it's choc-choc time. We'll just——'

'Where the hell have you been all weekend?' rasped a deeply familiar voice.

She looked up with a start, to see Jerard push himself forcefully away from his lounging position against the wall. Tony was obviously in awe of the dark man towering over them, and buried his face in Velvet's skirt.

'It's all right, Tony,' she soothed, bending down to swing him up into her arms. 'This man is a friend of Mummy's. See?' she gave a bright smile.'

'Don't go overboard, Velvet,' Jerard drawled. 'I might think you mean it.'

She flashed him a resentful glance. 'I'm trying to comfort my child—can't you see he's shy!'

He looked at the little boy in her arms, his eyes narrowed and enigmatic. 'Hello, Tony,' he said softly.

Tony eyed him warily, burying his face in Velvet's neck. 'Choc-choc,' he mumbled.

Jerard smiled. 'His shyness doesn't seem to have diminished his appetite!'

Velvet silently unlocked her flat door, taking Tony inside and sitting him on his booster chair before turning back to collect their cases. Jerard had already entered with them, putting them down in the passageway before closing the door behind him.

'Come in, won't you?' she said sarcastically, taking some chocolate out of her handbag and handing it to Tony as he sat at the kitchen table, his smile of glee softening her mood.

'I asked where you'd been.' Jerard stood in the kitchen doorway, dark and attractive in black fitted shirt and trousers.

She shot him another resentful glance. 'I've been away,' she snapped.

'I know that,' he said fiercely, shooting Tony a searching glance, but the little boy was intent on his chocolate, not at all interested in the heated conversation of the two adults. 'I want to know where,' Jerard rasped.

Velvet's eyes widened. 'I don't see what that has to do with you. You——'

'Don't you?' he interrupted dangerously soft. 'Don't you really? Well, let me tell you what it has to do with me, shall I? I called you when you got back from Miami because I had one hysterical little girl on my hands—I would have thought that much was obvious by the fact that you spoke to Vicki. The only way I could calm her down was by promising to bring her back to England immediately, and by letting her talk to you on the telephone straight away. For some reason you chose to put the phone down on me,' his eyes were narrowed, 'and then you childishly wouldn't take any more of my calls.'

'I—How is Vicki now?' she asked guiltily, knowing that his description of her behaviour being childish was an accurate one.

'She's with my mother—yes, I have one,' he mocked at her surprised expression. 'Vicki often stays with her, even before Tina died. But even my mother agrees with me that we've never seen Vicki quite so attached to anyone as she is to you.'

She licked her lips worriedly. 'You—you told your mother about me?'

'Only that Vicki had become friends with you in Fort Lauderdale.' His mouth twisted. 'Don't worry, Velvet, the past is dead and buried as far as I'm concerned, very dead and buried. But you knew the risk when you allowed Vicki to latch herself on to you, and you can't just walk away from that responsibility now that you're back in England and it suits you to do so.'

Velvet gasped. 'It doesn't *suit* me to at all! I'm as fond of Vicki as she seems to be of me, but my work in America was finished, and—and I had to get back to Tony.'

His harsh features softened as he looked at the now chocolate-covered little boy. 'He's a beautiful child,' he said softly. 'Very like you to look at.'

'Thank you,' she accepted awkwardly, moving to clean her son's face. 'All right,' she laughed once he was clean, 'you can go down now. Off you go and play with your toys.'

'Can I use your telephone?' Jerard asked tersely.

Velvet blinked up at him. 'I—Yes, yes, of course. It's in the lounge.'

'Thanks.' He strode off into the other room.

Velvet stood awkwardly in the kitchen, undecided about whether or not she should join Tony and Jerard in the lounge. Why shouldn't she, it was her home after all!

'Yes, Mother, it's me,' Jerard was saying patiently as Velvet entered the room. 'Yes, she's back,' he glanced fleetingly at Velvet as she sat down, her expression one of defiance. 'I'll be bringing her and her little boy back to tea,' he added.

Velvet gasped, sitting forward. 'You——'

'We'll be there in twenty minutes,' he said firmly before replacing the receiver. He looked at Velvet challengingly. 'You were saying?' he drawled.

'Yes, I was!' She stood up angrily, lowering her voice as Tony looked up worriedly from playing with his fire-engine. 'Tony and I aren't going anywhere with you,' she told him indignantly. 'We've only just got home.'

'From where?'

'You're very persistent,' she said tersely.

He raised his eyebrows. 'You've only just realised that?'

'No, I knew you were arrogant and bossy,' she snapped.

'So?'

'So . . .? Oh,' she realised he was still waiting for an answer to his question, 'I've been staying with my brother and his wife.'

'Is that the truth?' His eyes were narrowed.

Her eyes flashed deeply brown. 'Of course it's the truth! Why should I lie?'

Jerard shrugged. 'You tell me.'

'I wasn't lying!'

He nodded. 'Shall we get going, then?'

Her mouth set mutinously. 'I already told you——'

'Not even for Vicki?'

'That isn't fair,' she said defeatedly.

Jerard's expression was grim. 'Neither is letting a child become dependent on you and then just walking out on her.'

Velvet went very pale. 'I didn't do that——'

'The hell you didn't!' Jerard exploded. 'You didn't have to come to Disneyworld with us, you could have just let Vicki forget you. But you did come with us, and I'm not going to let you walk out on my daughter now. She's too vulnerable.'

Velvet bit her bottom lip. 'But I've only just got home. I—I'm not dressed to go out.' Her skirt and sun-top were casual in the extreme.

'You always look beautiful, and you know it,' he told her harshly.

'But—I—Tony's filthy,' she indicated his chocolate-smudged tee-shirt and shorts.

'Then change him,' Jerard shrugged. 'But do whatever you have to do quickly. My mother is expecting us.'

She scooped Tony up in her arms with an angry sigh, taking him into the bathroom and washing his face and hands again before changing him into a clean tee-shirt and denims, much to his indignation. He enjoyed nothing more than getting dirty, and disliked nothing more than being changed. She brushed his blond curls into some semblance of order, amazed at how angelic he could look when he had been washed and tidied.

Jerard was stretched out in a chair when she came out into the lounge, putting down the magazine he had been flicking through. 'It sounded like you were murdering him in there,' he said with amusement.

Her eyes flashed. 'He isn't the one I would like to murder,' she told him meaningly. 'Here,' she put Tony on his lap, 'I'm just going to change.' The yell she had been expecting from Tony never came as he gazed up in fascination at Jerard, totally captivated by this new man in his young life.

Jerard didn't look in the least put out either, holding Tony easily against him. 'You look all right as you are.'

'I am not going to your mother's dressed like this!'

'Why not?'

'Because—well, because I'm not,' she told him firmly. 'I won't be long.'

'You'd better not be,' he warned. 'Not if we're going to get to my mother's in the specified time.'

She glared at him before slamming into her bedroom,

angrily searching through the dresses in her wardrobe for something suitable to wear to meet Jerard's mother.

Oh God, if only she didn't love him so much! It had made her offhand and rude to him, and it threw this meeting with his mother out of all proportion. As far as Jerard was concerned, and indeed his mother, she was just a woman his daughter happened to be rather fond of.

Only she could no longer see it in that light, her love for Jerard making her want to make a good impression on his mother. Consequently she was longer than the allotted time, although there were no complaints from Jerard before or after she emerged from the bedroom, looking coolly beautiful in a pale lilac dress that shimmered about her slender body, her legs long and smooth in silky stockings, her hair a shining cap round her head.

Jerard raised his eyebrows at her changed appearance, although he made no comment, standing up with Tony still in his arms. 'Ready?'

'Yes,' she nodded. 'Shall I take Tony now?'

'He's fine with me, aren't you, Buster?' He strode out of the flat still carrying Tony.

Velvet hurriedly collected up a few toys for Tony to play with, stuffing them into a bag before hurrying after them. Jerard was already seated in a Jaguar, Tony jumping up and down in front of him as he played with the steering-wheel, although he reached over to unlock the back door for her.

He shrugged. 'It's the best I can do without a child seat.'

She took Tony into the back with her. 'Would you rather we followed behind in my car? I could drive myself back later that way.'

'You'll drive with me,' Jerard told her imperiously, starting the car engine. 'I'll drive you home later.'

'Oh, but——'

'I said I'll drive you.' He controlled the car as easily as he controlled the lives of those about him.

'God, you are bossy today!'

He glanced at her in the driving mirror. 'He's a handful, isn't he?' he smiled as Tony refused to sit still, clambering about all over her.

'Did you hear what I said?' she flashed. 'I said——'

'I heard you Velvet. And I'm not going to let you anger me, my mother just wouldn't understand. What do you do with Tony when you're working?' he frowned. 'Does he interfere with your career at all?'

Her mouth twisted into a bitter smile. 'Don't you mean does my career interfere with my bringing him up?' she taunted.

Jerard shook his head. 'If I'd meant that I would have said it. There's no reason why you shouldn't work and be a mother at the same time. It's no longer compulsory for a woman to stay at home when she has a child, in fact I think it's better if she doesn't. A woman doesn't stop being an individual just because she becomes a mother.' Once again he glanced at her in the mirror. 'You didn't expect that would be my attitude, did you?' he mused.

'No,' she admitted. 'But then I'm beginning to learn not to expect the expected where you're concerned.'

'I'll take that as a compliment,' he drawled. 'Although I doubt it was meant as one. So, how do you manage with Tony during the day?'

She shrugged. 'He mainly comes with me. Most of the time it's possible to do that. Occasionally I leave him with Simon's wife, but not very often. I wouldn't do the job if I felt it would harm Tony.'

'I know that,' Jerard said deeply. 'And at least this way the world hasn't lost a beautiful woman.'

'Thank you,' she accepted huskily, surprised they could hold such a normal conversation, but aware that

Jerard was being deliberately friendly to put her at her ease. 'Your mother—what's she like?'

'Sixty-eight years of age, grey hair, blue eyes, a complete darling, but don't tell her I said so.'

'She—she sounds—nice.'

Jerard laughed, a huskily attractive sound. 'She is, don't worry. Tony will love her, all children do. And she'll love him too.' He sobered, his expression suddenly harsh. 'She's quite disgusted with the fact that I haven't provided her with a grandson.'

'There's still time,' Velvet said awkwardly, hating the unknown woman who might one day be his wife and give him a son.

'No!' he denied forcefully. 'I don't ever intend to marry again. I haven't loved very wisely in my life so far,' he added abruptly.

She flushed, knowing that dig had been made at her. He considered that loving her had been an unwise thing to do. He couldn't have told her any more clearly that loving her in the first place had been a mistake, a mistake that was now rectified.

His mother's house was on the outskirts of London, one of the older houses set in its own grounds. Velvet was overwhelmed before she even stepped foot inside the gracious old house, the wood-panelled hallway leading up a wide flight of stairs to the second floor.

Jerard had again taken charge of Tony, something her son didn't seem to mind in the least. 'It gets worse,' he mocked at her awed expression. 'My mother has been collecting this junk for years.'

'This junk' turned out to be beautiful antique furniture, and what Velvet was sure were priceless pieces of china. It was a beautiful home, beautiful and gracious, like the woman who stood up as they walked into the drawing-room.

'Velvet!' Vicki jumped down from her seat at the

table where she had been working on a jigsaw puzzle, diverting Velvet's attention away from Jerard's mother as the little girl laughingly threw herself into her arms. 'Oh, Velvet, I missed you so!' she choked.

'I missed you too.' Velvet stroked Vicki's hair, holding her for several minutes before putting her away from her. 'But I'm here now,' she said brightly. 'And look who I've brought with me!' She took her son from Jerard's arms, putting him down on the floor beside Vicki. 'This is Tony.'

Vicki looked at him silently for a few minutes. 'He's small, isn't he?' she said.

'So were you once,' her father ruffled her hair. 'Take Tony into the kitchen and get him a biscuit while I introduce Velvet to your grandmother.'

Vicki took the little boy firmly by the hand, pulling him out of the room.

'They'll be all right,' Jerard assured Velvet as she anxiously watched their exit. 'Molly, my mother's housekeeper, will take care of them.' He took a firm hold of her elbow and took her over to his mother. 'Velvet, my mother, Sarah Daniels. Mother, this is Velvet Dale.'

His mother smiled warmly, a woman almost as tall as Jerard himself, with his strong features and blue eyes, although the latter were kind in this woman, and not cold like Jerard's. 'Velvet, you said,' her voice was warm and kind too. 'What a pretty name!'

'Thank you,' she accepted shyly.

'Very unusual,' Mrs Daniels nodded.

'Very,' she agreed.

'Please, sit down,' the other woman invited. 'Molly will bring in the tea now that you're here.'

Velvet glanced nervously at Jerard before sitting down on the sofa, hoping he would sit down beside her to give her support. He didn't. He sat in one of the armchairs, his long legs stretched out in front of him, a bored expression to his face.

As if on cue the housekeeper wheeled in the tea-trolley, smiling at Velvet before leaving the room again.

'Would you like to pour, Velvet? I may call you Velvet, I hope?' Sarah Daniels enquired politely.

'Of course,' she nodded.

Sarah Daniels held up arthritic hands. 'I'm afraid these don't work as well as they used to,' she explained the reason for asking Velvet to deal with the pouring of the tea.

She sat forward, pouring three cups of tea, adding milk and sugar at Mrs Daniels' request, automatically handing Jerard unsweetened tea with a slice of lemon.

'Oh,' she stopped in the process of giving it to him, frowning her puzzlement, 'I—er——'

'This is fine, Velvet.' He took the cup from her hand. 'Exactly as I like it.'

She blinked hard. 'But I—How did I know that?'

His smile openly mocked her. 'Guesswork?'

She flushed at his unmistakable sarcasm, and hastily took a sip of her own tea, burning her mouth in the process. Jerard's expression still mocked as she glanced up at him nervously. She had no idea how she had known the way he liked his tea, but it was obvious how he thought she had known. As far as Jerard was concerned she had just added to his conviction that she was lying about forgetting the past—their past.

'My son tells me the two of you met in Florida.' Mrs Daniels spoke again.

'Yes,' Velvet acknowledged tautly.

'I'm surprised at the extent to which Vicki is clinging to you. She doesn't usually take to people in this way.'

'I like her too,' Velvet said shyly.

'I was wondering——'

'Mother!' Jerard cut in abruptly. 'Any arrangement

Velvet and I make about Vicki will be made by us.'

'But I was only——'

'Mother!'

She was silent with effort. Velvet looked at the silent battle of wills that went on between mother and son. Jerard obviously beat his mother hands down.

'I would love to see Vicki at any time,' she said into the strained silence.

'Tomorrow?' Vicki asked eagerly as she and Tony came back into the room, both of them eating a chocolate biscuit.

'Not tomorrow,' her father refused before Velvet could speak. 'I'm sure Velvet has to work.'

'But Tony goes with her,' Vicki pouted.

'Tony is——'

'I think it will be all right, Jerard,' Velvet cut into his refusal firmly. 'I'm only going to finish off the photographs for Paul. I don't think he would mind Vicki coming with Tony and me.'

Vicki's face glowed. 'I really can go with you?'

Velvet looked at Jerard, noting his harsh disapproval. 'The final decision lies with your father.'

'Daddy?' She looked at him hopefully.

He sighed impatiently. 'If Velvet doesn't mind then neither do I.'

'I don't. I—No, Tony,' Velvet ordered as he made a beeline for Mrs Daniels' silky dress with his sticky fingers. 'No!' and she laughingly scooped him up into her arms.

Mrs Daniels stood up. 'I'll take him into the kitchen and wash his hands.' She took Tony into her arms. 'And you too, young lady,' she ordered her granddaughter. 'You have more cholcolate around your mouth than must have gone inside it! Come along,' she instructed briskly, taking them both out of the room.

Velvet looked nervously at Jerard, biting her bottom

lip as he scowled back at her.

'You don't have any sense at all, do you?' he rasped suddenly. 'Vicki will never let you go as long as you continue to encourage her.'

'Oh, I didn't——'

'You did, damn you,' he snapped, standing up to pace the room. 'Vicki has just begun her school holidays for the summer, if you aren't careful she'll want to be with you every day of it.'

'I was only trying to help.' She flushed. 'You said I had a responsibility, that——'

'Oh, shut up, Velvet,' he said tersely, pulling her roughly into his arms. 'Just shut up,' he groaned before his mouth came down on hers.

For the first time since their meeting a week ago Velvet kissed him willingly, her arms going up about his neck as she arched against him. The kiss gentled, as he slowly savoured the taste of her mouth, his hands softly caressing her back.

He raised his head, looking down at her with dazed blue eyes. 'Velvet?'

She looked up at him. 'Yes?'

'Nothing.' He put her firmly away from him, turning his back on her. 'My mother and the children will be back in a moment.'

And he didn't want his mother to see him kissing her! Her smile was forced as Mrs Daniels and the children returned, the latter noticeably cleaner. 'I think Tony and I should be going now,' Velvet suggested lightly, studiously avoiding looking at Jerard as she said it.

'Won't you stay to dinner?' Sarah Daniels invited.

She shook her head. 'I should get Tony home to bed soon. It's been a long day for him.'

'Of course. I—Jerard, what do you have on your mouth?' His mother touched a tissue to the side of his mouth.

'I'm not a child, mother,' he growled, flinching away.

'No, dear,' his mother smiled, her eyes twinkling merrily. 'But this plum shade really isn't your colour, Jerard,' she teased. 'Now on Velvet it looks lovely, but on you——'

'All right, mother,' his scowl increased. 'You've made your point. Let's go,' he told Velvet curtly, swinging Tony up into his arms, a Tony who no longer seemed surprised by the amount of new people he had met today.

'Can I come?' Vicki asked hopefully.

'Stay and keep Grandma company.' Jerard's voice softened as he spoke to his daughter. 'You'll be seeing Velvet tomorrow.'

'Yes,' she grinned, 'I will, won't I?'

'Nice and early,' Velvet warned. 'I'll call for you at eight o'clock.'

'I'll see that she's ready,' Mrs Daniels promised.

Velvet glanced apprehensively at Jerard during the drive to her home. He looked ready to explode! And she knew why, her mouth quirking into a smile as she remembered his anger when his mother had discovered the lipstick on his mouth.

'What's so damned funny?' he snapped suddenly.

She bit her lip guiltily. 'I——'

'Don't bother to answer. Just remember how funny you found this when my mother starts her infernal matchmaking. She happens to think I need a wife, and I have a feeling she's decided you might fit the role perfectly.'

It seemed that only Jerard was averse to the idea now, and she certainly didn't want to marry anyone who didn't love her.

CHAPTER SEVEN

VICKI was ready and waiting when she called for her the next morning, Jerard apparently having dropped her off at his mother's on his way to his office.

'I didn't realise,' she apologised to his mother. 'I thought Vicki was staying with you.' Mrs Daniels had persuaded her to stay for a cup of coffee, while Vicki and Tony played together on the floor.

'Only for the weekend.' Mrs Daniels was watching the children too. 'They get on well together, don't they?'

'Yes.' Velvet bit her lip, feeling that some explanation was necessary for yesterday. 'Mrs Daniels——'

'Sarah,' the older woman encouraged.

'About yesterday——'

'Yes,' Sarah Daniels sighed, 'I don't think you can add anything to what my son's already said.'

'Jerard—spoke to you?'

'At me,' the other woman corrected dryly.

Velvet looked down at her hands. 'I—What did he say?'

'All of it, or just the polite bits?'

Velvet gave a reluctant smile at the humour in Sarah Daniels' voice. 'Just the polite bits, I think.'

'Well, let me see. He told me not to interfere, not to jump to conclusions, and to mind my own business,' she revealed.

Velvet's eyes widened. 'Those were the polite bits?'

'Oh yes,' the other woman nodded.

'Oh.'

Sarah Daniels laughed. 'Jerard was always very blunt, even as a boy.'

127

Velvet couldn't imagine him ever being a little boy, Tony's age and vulnerable; she was sure that he must have been born arrogant and self-assured.

'I'll show you some photographs of him some time.' His mother seemed to guess her thoughts. 'I think you might find some of them rather amusing.'

'I might,' Velvet grinned. 'But I don't think Jerard would.'

'Pooh!' his mother dismissed. 'No one asked him. I'll sort them out and show them to you another time.'

The last statement gave the present arrangement a permanency that Velvet didn't have the time to disabuse at the moment; she rushed the children out to the car and drove quickly to Paul's studio.

'You're late,' he snapped as she breathlessly entered the studio. 'Good God,' he scowled as he saw the two children with her, 'this isn't a kindergarten, you know, Velvet.'

'Oh, shut up, Paul,' Carly told him, helping Velvet set the children's toys out on a table at the back of the room.

Velvet hurriedly changed into her first outfit, feeling much more comfortable here in the scanty shorts and top than she had on the Fort Lauderdale beach. 'I didn't think you would mind,' she told Paul, touching up her lipstick before going in front of the camera.

'That's the Daniels kid, isn't it?' Paul didn't answer her statement.

'Yes,' she blushed.

'Funny—Smile. Yes, that's it. Look down. Daniels didn't say anything—Wicked, Velvet. Look wicked. He didn't say anything about—Now look up. Lose the smile—about coming back to England.'

Luckily she was able to follow his conversation interspersed with his instructions. 'I believe it was a rather sudden decision.' She avoided looking at the camera, knowing Paul missed nothing through its lens.

'I'll bet it was,' he scorned.

'Paul——'

'Next outfit, Velvet,' he ordered abruptly.

She touched his arm. 'I'm sorry about the children.'

'It doesn't matter,' he shrugged. 'You know I like Tony, and Vicki seems a nice little kid. As long as they don't interfere with our work,' he added warningly.

'They won't,' she promised. 'Vicki will help keep Tony amused.'

The little girl did that very well, seeming happy herself as long as Velvet didn't go too far away. Mrs Daniels insisted they stay to tea when they returned to her house, although Velvet turned down the idea of dinner, sure that Jerard would be back before then to pick up Vicki.

'Can I come with you tomorrow too?' Vicki wanted to know.

Velvet thought of Jimmy Lance, the man she was modelling for tomorrow. Jimmy loved children, had a boy and girl of his own that he doted on. 'I think so,' she nodded agreement.

'Are you sure?' Mrs Daniels frowned.

'Yes,' Velvet smiled. 'Although it won't be possible all the time,' she added for Vicki's benefit.

In actual fact it wasn't possible on the Friday of that week. She was booked for a day of modelling lingerie, and she had to go out of town for it. When she explained the situation to Mrs Daniels she instantly offered to care for both Tony and Vicki for the day. Velvet had refused at first, but the other woman had been most insistent, and so finally she had agreed, dropping Tony off at the house at seven-thirty, before Jerard had even arrived with Vicki.

She had seen nothing of him this last week, usually managing to miss him by minutes as he dropped Vicki off at his mother's or picked her up. On Friday morning she wasn't so lucky.

Tony had clambered up on to the armchair that looked out on to the front of the house. 'Bicki,' he cried excitedly. 'Bicki!'

Knowing this was his version of Vicki's name Velvet felt her heart sink. If Vicki was here then it also followed that Jerard was too. 'Careful, darling!' She absentmindedly helped Tony down from the chair as he would have fallen in his excitement to get to Vicki, the two of them having become firm friends.

Vicki bounded in, closely followed by her father, Jerard looking very distinguished in the navy blue three-piece suit and contrasting lighter blue shirt. After that first hungry look Velvet turned away, knowing that hunger must be in her eyes and not wanting Jerard to see it.

'Velvet,' he greeted her abruptly. 'I understand you're going out of town today?'

She flushed at what she felt to be a rebuke. 'I do have to work,' she snapped. 'I warned you——'

'It was only a polite attempt at conversation, Velvet,' he interrupted coldly.

'Oh,' her flush deepened. 'I—I didn't realise.'

'No,' he sighed. 'Vicki hasn't been too much trouble to you this week?'

'No,' she replied tautly. 'I've enjoyed having her with me. Have you done anything about replacing Miss Rogers?' He had kept his word and sacked the other girl.

'Not yet. But if Vicki is too much for you——'

'She isn't. I told you, I enjoy having her with me. And so does Tony.' She looked down to where the children were already playing together on the carpet at their feet.

He nodded. 'Then you must allow me to repay your kindness,' his tone was stiff, totally lacking in warmth. 'Perhaps you and Tony would like to spend the day with us on Sunday?'

'I—Well, I——'

'Just say if it isn't convenient,' he cut in coolly. 'I'm sure Vicki and I will manage if you can't make it.'

Her mouth set angrily. 'We can make it,' she told him through gritted teeth.

'Good. I'll call for you both at ten.' He turned to kiss his mother on the cheek. 'See you later, Velvet,' he nodded distantly.

'Jerard,' she returned that nod.

She watched him as he kissed Vicki goodbye, absently bending to ruffle Tony's curls before leaving. She breathed easier once he had left, colour flooding her cheeks as she realised Sarah was watching her with open amusement.

'He may be my son,' Sarah chuckled, 'but he's a devil.'

'Yes,' Velvet agreed with feeling.

Sarah continued to smile. 'Shouldn't you be leaving yourself now?'

'Heavens, yes!' She made a hurried departure, surprised to find Jerard's car still parked outside.

His car window slowly wound down. 'How are you, Velvet?' he asked softly.

She frowned at his change of mood. 'I—I'm well.'

'Do you have to work today?'

'Of course. Why?'

He shrugged. 'I thought we could play truant together. But if you have to work . . .' He turned in his seat to start up the engine.

'I——' Velvet bit her lip, tempted beyond endurance. She wanted to go with Jerard, wanted desperately to be with him, but she had never not turned up for a booking. When Tony had been born she had been aware of the favour a lot of people did her by still giving her work, and she had repaid that kindness by never letting anyone down. 'Yes, I do have to work,' she said regretfully. 'I—I'm sorry.'

'It wasn't important.' Jerard's expression was remote.
'I'll see you on Sunday.'

Not important, he had said. Well, it was important to
her, the reason behind the invitation even more so.
'Why, Jerard?' she asked huskily. 'Why did you want to
take me out?'

'Your guess is as good as mine,' he dismissed harshly,
pressing the button to close the window, and the car
moved off with hardly a sound.

Velvet was cloaked in depression all day, having none
of her usual zest for work, so much so that Joyce finally
called a halt to the photographing.

You're supposed to look sexy, Velvet,' she com-
pained. 'That bra is supposed to drive men wild—although personally I think any red-blooded man would
prefer you without it,' she added dryly. 'Still, ours not
to reason why. Think sexy, Velvet. Think of some dishy
man you'd like to go to bed with.'

Jerard instantly sprang to mind, her expression unknowingly becoming provocative, her eyes love-drugged
as she thought of being made love to by him. He said
they had been good in bed together, that their love had
been special, that she had haunted his days and invaded
his nights for two years. Oh, how she ached for that
closeness to him she couldn't even remember!

'Beautiful!' Joyce lowered her camera. 'That was fantastic, Velvet. You just sizzled!'

Colour stained her cheeks. 'I—You took the
pictures?'

'Mm,' Joyce nodded. 'He must be some man.'

'He is,' Velvet admitted huskily.

'But you're keeping him hidden, hmm?' Joyce
teased.

Velvet looked at the other woman. Would Jerard find
Joyce attractive? A lot of men did, she was beautiful

enough to have been a model herself with her long black hair and flashing blue eyes, but she preferred to be behind the camera rather than in front of it. Yes, Jerard would probably find her very attractive, and jealousy shot through her just at the thought of it.

She didn't know whether she was pleased or upset when she saw the Jaguar parked outside Sarah Daniels' house. Jerard was here! She wasn't late, it was only four-thirty, so he must be early. And after the thoughts she had had of him earlier she felt embarrassed about facing him. Not that he could possibly know about them, but she did, and it still made her blush.

She forgot all about it with the sight that met her eyes when she went into the lounge. Jerard was lying on his back on the carpeted floor, Tony lying on his chest, chuckling so hard Velvet thought he was going to burst with merriment. Vicki lay on the floor next to her father, enjoying this game as much as Tony was.

'Good evening, Velvet,' Sarah smiled at the antics going on on the floor.

'Hello,' Velvet smiled too.

Jerard stood up, Tony still beaming in his arms. 'You look tired.' His eyes were narrowed.

'Mum—Mum!' Tony reached out his arms towards her, burrowing into her throat as she cuddled him to her.

'Thank you, darling,' she smiled tremulously at her son. 'At least you know how to say hello nicely.' She flashed a look of dislike in Jerard's direction.

His mouth twisted into a mocking smile. 'I know how to say hello nicely too,' he drawled, his hand coming out behind her nape to pull her towards him before he kissed her hard on the mouth.

'Oh!' she gasped, her face bright red as she looked pointedly at his mother.

Tony struggled to go down at that moment, so at least she was able to bend down and hide some of her embarrassment. Why had Jerard done that, especially in front of his family!

Jerard turned to his mother, dabbing at his mouth with a snowy white handkerchief. 'What do you think of this shade?' he mocked.

'Better than the plum.' Her eyes twinkled with humour.

'I thought so,' he grinned.

Velvet looked away. 'Tony and I had better be going now,' she said awkwardly, looking only at Sarah. 'Thank you for taking care of him for me.'

'Jerard did that, my dear. He came back this afternoon and took them to the park.'

'Oh. I see. I—But how?' she frowned. 'You don't have a child seat in your car.' She could imagine Tony leaping about all over the back seat with Vicki unable to control him.

'I had one put in this morning after you agreed to spend the day with Vicki and me on Sunday,' Jerard told her casually.

'You——? You didn't have to do that!' she gasped heatedly.

'It's safer,' he dismissed.

'Yes, but——'

'Stop arguing, woman,' he growled, 'and sit down. You aren't going anywhere until you've had some tea. Sit,' he ordered as she hesitated.

She did so, resentfully. 'What did your last dog die of?' she snapped.

'Old age,' he drawled.

'I'm surprised,' she scorned.

Jerard's eyes narrowed. 'Would you like another lesson in obedience?'

'No, thank you!' She couldn't mistake the threat in his voice.

'Then sit there and rest,' he instructed before striding out of the room.

Velvet drew an angry breath, her attention not completely on the game of Snakes and Ladders Vicki had persuaded her into. How dared Jerard treat her like this in front of his mother? How dared he treat her like this at all!

She was about ready to get up and leave when Jerard came back into the room carrying a tea tray. Even doing such a mundane task he looked vitally attractive, having changed out of the three-piece suit some time during the day into a black sweat-shirt and black denims. But why was he doing such a mundane task, why get *her* tea?

'I thought I told you to rest,' he said sternly. 'Play with your grandma, Vicki, Velvet's had a hard day.'

'Okay,' his daughter accepted goodnaturedly, collecting up her board and dice, and taking Tony with her. He seemed to have become her shadow lately, chanting her name monotonously when they were at home.

'Will you stop being sarcastic to me!' Velvet muttered under her breath to Jerard.

His eyebrows rose. 'Who's being sarcastic?' He put the tray down on a small coffee-table and pulled it over in front of her. 'We've already had ours,' he explained as she looked questioningly at the single cup on the tray, the small plate of cakes. 'And there was no sarcasm intended—I know how hard models work.'

'Do you?' she snapped, her mouth tight. 'How many of your girl-friends have been models?'

'Only one,' he revealed tightly, sitting down at her feet.

'I suppose—Oh. You mean me . . .' she realised dully.

'Yes. Drink your tea, you'll feel better.'

This time she didn't resent his autocratic behaviour, but drank the tea gratefully, although she didn't touch the cakes, very conscious of Jerard sitting so close to her.

An outsider could be forgiven for completely misunderstanding this situation, for thinking that she and Jerard were husband and wife, and that Vicki and Tony were their children, with the doting grandmother looking on. For a moment Velvet allowed herself the luxury of basking in that dream—until she became aware of Jerard watching her. She flushed, looking away from his mesmerising blue eyes.

'I really do have to go now,' she said briskly. 'Tony has to have his bath, and I have to prepare our dinner.'

'You work too hard,' Jerard scowled. 'You should have a nanny to care for Tony.'

'We aren't all as rich as you,' she scorned. 'Besides, I like taking care of him myself.' She looked up to see her son yawning tiredly. 'Bed for you, little man,' and she held out her arms to him, laughing as he ran into them.

'I'll carry him out to the car for you,' Jerard stood up to offer.

'There's no need——'

'I know that, but I'm going to do it anyway,' he said firmly. 'Stop being so damned independent.'

'I'm not——'

'You are,' he told her fiercely. 'My mother told me how much you fought against leaving Tony here today.'

'I didn't want to be a burden——'

'You aren't, and neither is Tony. You've had Vicki all week, with no complaints, the least we could do is care for Tony for one day. Surely you realise how much my mother loves him?'

'Yes,' she acknowledged huskily.

'And you aren't sure that's a good thing, are you?'

'No,' she didn't attempt to prevaricate. 'This whole situation is getting very complicated.'

Jerard shook his head. 'It isn't complicated at all, it's very simple when you think about it.'

Velvet gave him a sharp look. 'What do you mean?'

Tony chose that moment to yawn once again, Jerard's harsh features relaxing as he looked down at him. 'He really is very tired. You'd better get him home.'

She gave him an impatient glance. 'That's what I've been trying to do for the last hour.'

'My, you are snappy today,' he taunted.

'And you're as arrogant as usual!'

'Glad you aren't disappointed,' he grinned.

She was never that around him; she was charged with excitement, sexually aware of him with every fibre of her body, but never ever disappointed.

She blushed as she realised his mother must be wondering what they were talking about so intently, not that the other woman seemed to mind; she was smiling at them indulgently. Jerard had been proved right about his mother's matchmaking; she never lost an opportunity to extol the virtues of her son, and she had taken great pleasure in showing Velvet the promised photographs of Jerard in his youth. They had been fascinating photographs, Jerard as a baby right through to his wedding day.

Tina Daniels had been a delicate woman to look at, very blonde, with a beautifully elfin face, her figure very slender. Sarah had told her that the photographs were ten years old, but even so Jerard had changed little; he was tall and handsome, his hair perhaps worn a little shorter, but otherwise he looked the same, a look of pride in his smiling blue eyes as he looked down at his bride.

Velvet had been racked with jealousy at the sight of that picture, even more so of the photographs that followed—Jerard and Tina on holiday, Jerard holding Vicki as a baby, Jerard playing with Vicki as she grew through the different stages of babyhood.

She had left Sarah's house feeling very depressed that evening, resenting any life Jerard had had before she had known him.

And she was just as depressed this evening as she drove off with a casual wave of her hand. She couldn't understand Jerard at all. They hadn't seen each other all week, and this morning he had treated her almost like a stranger, this evening his mood had turned around completely, teasingly flirtatious. He was a complex man, and it would take a lifetime to know him. But she didn't have a lifetime; she might not have any time at all.

Saturday was spent with Janice and Simon, the latter very curious as to who 'Bicki' was.

'Vicki Daniels,' Velvet supplied reluctantly.

His eyebrows rose. 'Any relation to Jerard Daniels?'

'His daughter.'

'Oh.'

'Don't say "oh" like that!' she flashed. 'I've just been looking after her until her father can find a replacement nanny for her.' Not strictly true, but she was sure Jerard would eventually replace Faye Rogers.

'Tony obviously likes her,' Simon observed dryly.

'Yes.'

'And do you still like her father?'

'Simon——'

'You didn't mention that he would be coming back to England.'

'I didn't know myself,' she defended. 'He—he just arrived on the doorstep.'

'With his daughter.'

'Well—no. But I saw her later.'

Simon began to laugh at her discomfort 'Purely platonic, is it?'

'It isn't funny,' Velvet snapped. 'I'm involved, and I'm not sure it's what I want.'

'You don't?'

'Not just as another playmate for Vicki, no.'

His mouth quirked. 'You would rather be a playmate for the father, hmm?'

'Simon——'

'Calm down,' he chuckled. 'And stop taking a man's simple pleasures from him. I like teasing you.'

'Simple is right,' she scorned. '"Simple Simon"! No, Simon,' she backed away as he got up from his lounger chair in the garden and started coming threateningly towards her, 'I didn't mean it!' she screamed as he threw her over his shoulder and marched her over to the hedgerow. 'Traitor!' she accused Tony as he chuckled uproariously. 'Simon, put me down,' she pleaded. 'My dress has ridden right up my legs! Simon, please!'

'All right.' He began to lower her down into the hedge.

'No, Simon!' she begged, clutching him tightly around the waist from behind. 'Simon, I'm starting to go dizzy,' she warned, as the upside-down world started to spin.

'That's why I'm putting you down.'

'Not in the hedge! I'm sorry,' she cried frantically. 'I'm sorry!'

'Need any help?' offered a familiar voice.

The world suddenly spun back into focus, and even upside-down she recognised Jerard with Janice. 'Put me down, Simon,' she begged in a fierce whisper, pulling ineffectually at her dress. 'Simon!' She would die of embarrassment in a moment.

'My husband Simon, Mr Daniels,' Janice introduced. 'And of course you know Velvet,' she added with amusement.

To Velvet's everlasting shame Simon shook hands with Jerard with her still thrown over his shoulder, the long expanse of her bare legs clearly visible. 'Nice to meet you, Mr Daniels,' he greeted goodnaturedly.

'Simon!' she groaned her dismay.

'Did you want something?' She wasn't able to see the wink he shot at Janice and Jerard.

'If you don't put me down I'll—I'll——'

'Yes?'

'Please put me down,' she choked.

'You only had to ask nicely.' He swung her back to the ground, a huge grin on his face.

She straightened her dress, too embarrassed to look up, sure that her pink lacy panties must have been visible as well. 'I'd been doing that for the last five minutes,' she muttered.

'Funny, I didn't hear you,' her brother said with feigned innocence.

She glared at him before looking awkwardly at Jerard. To make matters worse his grin was as wide as Simon's, convincing her that she had been right about her panties showing. 'Did you want something, Jerard?' she snapped.

'Not particularly,' came his infuriating reply.

She only just stopped herself from asking what he was doing here then. 'Is Vicki all right?' She couldn't keep the anxiety out of her voice.

'Fine,' he nodded, his faded denims and navy blue shirt casual in the extreme.

'Your mother?'

'Is also fine.'

'Oh.' She frowned her consternation. What was he doing here?

'I'm fine too, in case you're interested,' he drawled mockingly.

'Come inside and have a beer,' Simon invited.

'Thanks,' Jerard accepted, much to Velvet's chagrin.

She didn't even question how he had known where Simon lived, just as she hadn't questioned how he had known her address and telephone number. Men like Jerard, rich and powerful, could always find out what they wanted to know. But *why* was he here?

'Nice,' Janice smiled once Simon and Jerard had disappeared into the house to get their beers.

'Yes.' Velvet still frowned.

'Is he staying to lunch?'

'No!' her voice was sharp. 'And don't you dare ask him.'

She tensed as the two men emerged from the house once again, Tony clinging to Jerard's hand. She hadn't even realised her son had followed them! It gave her a curious lump in her throat to see how fond he was of Jerard.

'I've asked Jerard to lunch,' Simon told them happily.

'That will be nice,' Velvet said in a stilted voice. She would kill her brother later, but right now she would have to make the best of the situation.

Jerard's mocking blue eyes over the top of his beer can seemed to tell her that he knew exactly what she was thinking. And he probably did! The man seemed to be able to read her mind most of the time.

'But I can't stay,' he drawled, his eyes taunting her now. 'I have to collect Vicki from my mother's.'

'That's a shame,' Simon said with genuine regret. 'Perhaps another time?'

'I hope so,' Jerard nodded. He finished his beer in one thirsty swallow. 'I'd better be going now.'

'Come again, any time,' Janice invited.

'I'd like to.' He gave her a warm smile before going down on his haunches to Tony. 'I have to go now, Buster,' he told him gently, holding him briefly in his arms before standing up again. 'I'll see you in the morning, Velvet.'

'I—Yes.' She watched as he walked off, still dazed by this lightening visit.

Tony ran after him. 'D—D—Da—Daddy!' he called desperately as Jerard didn't notice him.

Jerard stiffened, slowly turning. 'Tony...!' he groaned, sweeping the little boy up against his chest, holding him tightly.

Velvet was very pale, walking over to them on shaky legs. 'I—I'm sorry,' she said weakly. 'I don't know why he said that. I—He only usually says Mum and Bicki. I can't understand——'

'It's all right, Velvet,' he dismissed huskily. 'He probably got it from Vicki yesterday. He's at an age where he picks things like that up easily.'

Maybe so, but he had never done anything this embarrassing before. She felt like running away and hiding. 'Yes, but he can't call you "Daddy",' she insisted firmly.

'I don't mind,' he shrugged.

'I do. This can't continue, Jerard. Our children are becoming confused about the whole situation.' She took the willing Tony out of his arms, a Tony who had no idea of the awkwardness he had just caused, grinning at them widely.

'I agree,' Jerard nodded.

She bit her lip. 'Then you think we should stop meeting?' Heavens, what was she saying!

'It's a thought,' he nodded.

'Oh.' She swallowed hard. 'Then tomorrow is off?'

'I didn't say that. No, I think tomorrow's plans should stand. We can sort out other arrangements from there. All right?'

'All right,' she nodded, just relieved to have this extra time with him. What on earth was she doing, suggesting they didn't meet again!

This time Jerard managed to get away without any protest from Tony. Velvet's face was scarlet as she turned to face Simon and Janice.

'I liked him,' Simon told her softly.

'I did too,' Janice added.

Velvet could have hugged them both in that moment for ignoring the gaffe Tony had made. Her brother liked to tease her, he always had, but he was sensible enough to realise Jerard Daniels was no longer a teasable subject.

Jerard arrived promptly at ten the next morning, Vicki jumping up and down excitedly at his side. Tony was almost as bad, as the two of them sat in the back of the car together, making for a very noisy drive.

'Did you bring a costume, Velvet?' Vicki sat forward to ask.

'No,' she frowned. 'Will I need one?'

'Daddy and I usually picnic at a lake and then swim later.'

'Oh.'

'Not today, Vicki,' Jerard cut in. 'I thought we could picnic in a park somewhere. Tony's still a little young for swimming.'

'Of course he is,' she grinned, not at all minding missing this treat if it were for Tony. 'Will there be swings and things? I could push him on them. Not very hard,' she added in her most grown-up voice, 'because he's still only little.'

'As if she's so big herself,' Jerard mused as his daughter went back to playing with Tony, their contented chuckles soon coming from the back.

'Talking of bathing costumes,' Velvet's mouth quirked, 'I hope the ones I was modelling in Florida aren't actually for going in the water?'

He frowned. 'I believe so.'

'Then you're going to get a lot of complaints.' She explained about her dip in the sea and Paul's reaction when she came out. 'It was very embarrassing,' although she could smile about it now.

'You mean you and Paul haven't been lovers?' he rasped.

'Certainly not!' She stiffened indignantly. 'It's Paul and Carly who are lovers. They've lived together for over a year.'

'And before that?'

'Before that I was married to Anthony and expecting Tony!'

'And before that there was just me.' His mouth twisted.

'Yes,' she choked.

'No one else since Anthony?'

'No! Why are you asking me all these questions?' she cried her anguish.

'Curiosity,' he shrugged.

Her eyes flashed. 'Then take your curiosity somewhere else!' she snapped. 'I'm not going to answer any more questions.'

'I'm not going to ask any,' he taunted. 'You've told me all I wanted to know.'

'I'm so glad! Am I allowed to pry into your sex life?' she whispered fiercely.

'Go ahead,' he shrugged.

Trust him to turn the tables on her! She had expected him to tell her to mind her own business, now she had no choice but to pursue the subject, no matter what pain it gave her to find out about the other women in his life.

'Well?' she prompted.

'Well what?'

Her mouth compressed angrily. 'How many women?'

'In my lifetime or lately?'

'In your lifetime!' She might as well know it all so that she could torture herself with it when she lay awake tonight in her bed thinking of him—as she had every night since their meeting.

'Now let me see, there was Barbara, and Celia, and——'

'I don't want a list of names, just the number!'

'That I've actually slept with, or that I've just been out with?'

'Slept with,' she said tightly.

'Maybe twenty or so.'

'Twenty!' she gasped. Heavens, it was a harem!

Jerard shrugged. 'Well, you have to take into account that I was married for ten years, and believe it or not I was faithful to my wife until I met you.'

'But twenty is so many!'

He gave her a sideways glance. 'Does it bother you?'

Yes, it bothered her. All those other women—no, not *other* women, she was probably counted amongst that number. The realisation made her feel sick. How far down the list did she come?

'Velvet?'

'Yes?'

'Good God, girl, I'm thirty-nine, not nineteen,' he said in exasperation.

'Are we nearly there?' Her tone was brittle. 'I'm sure the children must be getting hungry.'

'I am,' Vicki chimed in, breaking the tension that had sprung up between the two adults. 'I bet Tony is too.'

'Okay,' her father laughed. 'The next pretty spot we come to, hmm?'

As far as he was concerned that highly personal conversation might as well not have taken place. He chased Vicki and Tony as Velvet laid the picnic out on a blanket Jerard's housekeeper had provided. There were several other people picnicking in this pretty part of Hampshire, and she knew that to them the four of them must look like a typical happy family unit.

Velvet was so miserable she couldn't raise any enthusiasm for the food, although the other three had no lack of appetite. Tony, always a fussy eater, had never eaten as well as he did when he was with Vicki.

There were no swings in the spot Jerard had stopped at, so they played another game of Chase instead, Tony finally having to be put in the back of the car for a nap. Vicki sat on the front seat to keep him company, and it was no surprise to Velvet that the little girl fell asleep too. Vicki looked so vulnerable when she was asleep, more like the shadowed little girl she had first been in Florida.

'She's getting better,' Jerard told Velvet when she joined him on the blanket beneath the huge oak tree they had used as shade against the sun while they ate.

'She is?' She wouldn't look at him, her trouser-clad knees drawn up under her chin as she watched a dog from one of the other parties as he chased a football around the trees.

'No tantrums since we got back from Florida.'

She shrugged, still watching the dog. 'Maybe she just prefers England. Her grandmother is here, and——'

'And you and Tony,' he put in deeply.

'Not for much longer,' she reminded him jerkily, tears shimmering in her dark almond-shaped eyes. 'You said we weren't to meet again after today.'

'No,' he shook his head, 'I didn't say that at all. I said we would have to make other arrangements. I think now is the time to do that. Do you have any idea why I called to see your brother yesterday?'

'None,' she frowned; the incident still bothered her, especially the part where Tony had called him 'Daddy'.

Jerard's gaze was unflinching as she looked at him. 'I thought that he and your sister-in-law should meet me before I asked you to marry me.'

'Before you——!' She swallowed hard, sure she couldn't have heard him correctly. 'What did you say?' she croaked.

He stood up forcefully, his profile turned away from her. 'Surely you can see it's the only solution,' he said tautly.

'Solution?' she gasped, all hope leaving her. This wasn't a marriage proposal made out of love or needing, but one of expediency.

'Tony needs a father, and Vicki needs a mother,' Jerard told her abruptly.

'And you and I?' she cried. 'What do we need?'

He drew a ragged breath. 'We aren't really the important ones in this. Well?' he turned to look at her, his gaze piercing. 'What's your answer?'

CHAPTER EIGHT

WHAT was her answer? What could her answer be to a marriage proposal put in such coldly blunt terms?

And yet it *was* a marriage proposal, of sorts. All she had to do was say yes, and she would become Jerard's wife, something she wanted with all her heart, albeit a marriage of convenience for their children's sake. Jerard had loved her once, he might do again once she was his wife.

'If you need time to think about it——'

'No!' her denial was sharp.

'No, you won't marry me, or no, you don't need time?' His voice was harsh.

'I—I'm not sure.' If she appeared too eager he would guess that she loved him, would know she would die rather than give him up.

'What's it going to take to make you sure?' he rasped, his expression remote.

Velvet licked her suddenly dry lips. 'Maybe I do need a little time. After all,' she added hastily, 'it's a big decision to make.'

'You needn't think I'll stop you working,' he told her in that cold, emotionless voice. 'You already know my opinion on working mothers. And you won't have to have Vicki and Tony with you all the time, I'll get a nanny for them both.'

'No! I mean—I don't want Tony to have a nanny, Vicki either for that matter. If it's all the same to you I think I would rather give up my work as a model and care for them at home. I've always wanted to have a try at designing clothes instead of wearing them, and I—I could do that at home.'

Jerard shrugged. 'It's up to you. You don't have to work at all if you would prefer not to, I just wanted to make it plain that I wouldn't stop you doing anything you want to do.'

'Thank you.' She looked down at her hands clenched about her knees, relaxing them as she saw how white her knuckles were. 'Perhaps I could let you know tomorrow?'

'Take all the time you want,' he dismissed. 'There's no rush.'

Having made the suggestion he now seemed in no hurry to have an answer. He was maybe even changing his mind! 'Tomorrow,' Velvet repeated jerkily. 'I'll definitely let you know tomorrow.'

'That's fine,' he shrugged.

'I'll call you,' she added firmly.

'I'll be out of town all day. I'll come round in the evening.'

'All right,' she nodded.

They were like two strangers, not a couple contemplating marriage! But it wasn't really to be a marriage, just a question of living together to give their children two parents.

And it was the ideal solution to the problem, Tony's growing dependence on Jerard was evidence of that, and Vicki's affection for her was unquestionable. Then why did she feel so damned miserable!

She had felt miserable about parting from Jerard and perhaps never seeing him again, and now she felt even more miserable that he had asked her to marry him. Maybe that was because he hadn't asked her to be a wife to him but a mother to his daughter. This marriage was to be a deal—a mother for Vicki, and a father for Tony. And yet she already knew what her answer was going to be, already knew she was going to accept.

Acting normally in front of Vicki and Tony for the rest of the day proved a great strain, but somehow she managed to get through it, although she was glad to get back to her flat that evening and put Tony to bed.

How would a marriage between her and Jerard turn out? How could it turn out, with her wanting him so desperately? Wouldn't she just be making her own living hell?

She knew the answer to all these questions, and yet her answer to Jerard tomorrow would still be the same. She wanted to marry him.

She didn't have a booking the next day, so she telephoned Simon and asked him if he could come over. She needed to talk to him, to get his opinion, even if the decision had already been made. He promised to come over in his lunchbreak.

She provided him with lunch, feeding Tony while they talked. 'So what do you think?' she asked anxiously once she had explained the situation to him.

'What do *you* think?'

Velvet bit her lip. 'I'm going to accept.'

'I thought so,' her brother nodded.

'Well?'

'What do you want me to say?' he shrugged.

'Do you think I'm doing the right thing?'

'Do you?'

'No,' she sighed.

'But you're going to do it anyway.'

'Yes.'

'Because you love him.'

'Yes.'

'Then you have your answer,' Simon said gently.

'But he doesn't love me,' she cried. 'He did once, but he doesn't now.'

'Did he tell you that?'

'Yes.' In Florida Jerard had been very explicit about

his change of feelings towards her.

'Then maybe you shouldn't accept.'

'But I want to!'

Simon bit his lip thoughtfully. 'What do you want me to say, Velvet? Yes, go ahead, it doesn't matter that he doesn't love you, that he just wants a mother for his daughter?'

'Tony will be getting a father too.'

'Yes,' he agreed heavily.

Her expression was one of pain. 'Do you think I'm being disloyal to Anthony?'

'Good God, no,' came his ready denial. 'He would be the first one to want to see you happy. But will you be happy with Jerard Daniels?'

'I have to try,' she sighed, knowing she wouldn't be happy with*out* him. 'Maybe it won't work out, but I have to try.'

'Because of the children?'

'No, because of me. And because of Jerard too. I'm sure I could make him happy, if he would let me. We were in love once, we could be again.'

Simon nodded. 'Love doesn't usually die completely. Sometimes it gets forgotten, but it doesn't die.'

Her mouth twisted. 'And I certainly did that. I don't think Jerard will ever forgive me for that.'

'It wasn't your fault,' her brother said indignantly.

'No,' she acknowledged softly.

Her brother looked regretfully at his watch. 'I have to get back to work now. Why don't you come over this evening and we can discuss it some more?'

'I told Jerard I would give him my answer tonight,' she blushed.

His eyebrows rose. 'He hasn't given you much time to think about it.'

'Tonight was my idea,' she admitted huskily, with a rueful smile. 'I would have said yes yesterday only I didn't want to look too eager.'

Simon stood up to leave. 'Just don't make the wedding this week,' he teased lightly. 'I can't get the time off.'

'Oh, I do love you!' She hugged him tightly to her.

'That's what big brothers are for.' He smoothed her hair.

'Do you think I ought to see if Mum and Dad would like to come over, and Nigel and Jenny, of course?'

'You'll get shot if you don't ask them,' he warned.

'I feel a bit embarrassed about telling them. The last time they came over was for my wedding to Anthony.'

Simon shook his head. 'Mum and Dad came back for Anthony's funeral too.'

'Oh yes,' she remembered dully.

'Hey, come on!' her brother chided. 'You should think only happy thoughts today.'

By the time Jerard arrived that evening she didn't seem to have had a single one. To make matters worse he was alone. Somehow she had expected Vicki to be with him.

'She's spending the night with my mother,' he answered her jerky query. 'And Tony's in bed, I presume?'

'Yes,' she said huskily.

She hadn't thought they would be alone this evening, sitting nervously on the edge of her chair, glad that she had changed into the rust-coloured knee-length dress; Jerard's own appearance was impeccable in a grey pin-striped suit and white shirt.

'I was late getting back from Birmingham.' Once again he seemed aware of her thoughts, reaching up to remove his tie and unbutton the top button to his shirt. 'I came straight here.'

'Have you had dinner?'

'I'll eat later,' he dismissed.

Velvet stood up, tall and slender, her hair like a red-gold nimbus round her head, unknowingly provocative in the figure-hugging dress. 'I'll get you something,' she offered, glad of the opportunity to be busy. 'Would a ham omelette and salad be all right?'

'Fine. But there's no need.' He sat back in the chair, his eyes closed, lines of weariness about his eyes.

Her heart went out to him. 'Wouldn't you rather go to bed? I mean—I—You look tired!' Her face was fiery red. What an idiot she was!

Jerard didn't even open his eyes. 'I'm aware of the fact that that wasn't a proposition, Velvet,' he drawled sleepily. 'You've made your opinion on that subject very clear.'

'Yes. Well, I—I'll go and get you something to eat.' She made a hasty escape to the kitchen, her hands up to her cheeks to hide her fiery cheeks.

She was making a complete fool of herself, acting like a stupid schoolgirl, not like a woman who had been married once and was now contemplating the married state for a second time. Jerard must think she was a prize idiot! She must pull herself together, act the sophisticated woman she was supposed to be.

She half expected Jerard to be asleep when she went back into the lounge with the tray containing food. But he wasn't; he was sitting back smoking a cigarette, his jacket and waistcoat to his suit removed and thrown casually across the back of a chair.

He stubbed the cigarette out at her entrance, getting up to come over to the dining-room table where she laid out his meal. 'I could have eaten when I got home,' he said as he sat down.

'I enjoyed doing it.' She couldn't look at him, moving out of his way as quickly as she could, too vibrantly aware of his masculinity, the sensual smell of his body and aftershave.

For all his protests he ate the meal with obvious enjoyment, insisting on helping her clear everything away again.

'Did you talk to Simon today?' he asked once they had returned to the lounge, Velvet seated in an armchair, he on the sofa. His expression had seemed to mock her choice of seat, but the derision was quickly masked.

Her almond-shaped eyes opened wide. 'How did you know I was going to?'

Jerard shrugged. 'He's your brother, it's only natural to assume you would want to discuss my suggestion with him.'

'Did you talk it over with your mother?' she flashed, resentful of the way he could guess her every movement. He was as much of an enigma now as he had been two weeks ago when they first met.

'You wouldn't be marrying my mother,' he said haughtily.

'Does Vicki know?'

'I didn't see any point in raising her hopes when I have no idea what your answer is going to be.'

Velvet licked her lips nervously. 'I—It's yes.'

His eyes narrowed. 'Yes, you'll marry me?'

'Yes,' she nodded.

He was very tense, sitting forward in his seat. 'Are you sure you've thought this over carefully?'

'Yes.' Her hands moved nervously together.

Jerard shook his head. 'I don't think I explained the situation properly yesterday.'

'You explained it very well,' she choked. 'Vicki needs a mother and Tony needs a father.'

'And I need a wife!'

Her eyes widened, her breathing suddenly shallow. 'A wife . . .?'

'Yes.' He stood up forcefully, pacing the room. 'You expected it to be a marriage of convenience, didn't you?'

he rasped. 'You in your bed, me in mine. Only no marriage I have is going to be like that again.'

Velvet swallowed hard, frowning. 'Again?'

'Yes—again!' he ground out fiercely. 'For God's sake don't pull that act on me now, Velvet. You know damn well that after Vicki was born Tina abhorred sex, that I lived a sham of a marriage until Vicki was four years old and I just couldn't take it any more. And I won't take it in any marriage we have either. If you marry me you sleep with me. If the thought of that puts you off the idea then you only have to say so and I'll get out.'

'I—It—I——' She stood up, turning away.

'Do you need more time?' His hands came down on her shoulders, spinning her round to face him, his eyes narrowed as he took in her pale features. 'Is it that much of a shock?' his voice gentled. 'Platonic marriage went out with the suffragettes, Velvet?' he prompted, worried at her continued silence.

What he was proposing wasn't a shock at all. She welcomed the suggestion. She had imagined them living in the same house like strangers, but surely if they were sharing the same bed it wouldn't be like that. Surely no man could stay aloof when he made love to you?

'Velvet?' he shook her gently. 'If the idea is that distasteful to you——'

'It isn't!' she cut in sharply. 'I just thought—You didn't say——'

'No—well, it was a little difficult trying to talk about such things yesterday. I was very conscious of the children. My daughter has busy little ears,' he added dryly.

She frowned. 'Is this the reason you wanted to know if I'd had any lovers?'

'Yes,' he rasped.

'And if I had?'

'I'd want you anyway!' he groaned. 'Oh, God, Velvet, don't you know I'm going quietly out of my mind!' His head lowered and his mouth claimed hers.

Her head tilted right back, returning the pressure of his lips, hers opening eagerly when the tip of his tongue slid along the edge of her lips to deepen the kiss. She arched against him, her fingers in the dark hair at his nape as the hardening of his thighs told her he was already aroused.

She felt the zip to her dress slowly slide down her back, raising no protest as Jerard slid the dress down to the floor, leaving her in her slip and bra, a willing victim to his experienced caresses.

With his mouth at her throat he slipped his hand beneath the lacy material of her bra, capturing her breast in his palm, his fingers gently massaging. Velvet trembled against him, her hands beneath his unbuttoned shirt.

'Are you going to let me love you?' he moaned.

'I don't think I can stop you,' she replied breathlessly as he caressed the hardness of her nipple.

He moved to look down at her, his caresses stopping. 'You can stop me, Velvet. You only have to say no.'

She was lost in the sensuous warmth of his eyes, a deep flush to his hard cheeks. She shook her head. 'I can't.'

'Are you going to marry me?' he asked softly.

'Yes,' she nodded.

'Then I'll say no for you,' he said firmly, bending to pick up her dress and help her put it back on. 'This time I can wait until we're married.'

She couldn't, she wanted him now. But Jerard was already turning away to button his shirt, the mood was broken. Velvet shivered as she fought down the impulse to plead with him to make love to her. They would be married soon, and then she would be able to share his bed every night. Surely they would attain some form of emotional closeness from their physical relationship? At the moment that was her only hope.

The wedding was set for a month's time, giving her family time to get over from Australia, and also for them to make all the arrangements that suddenly seemed necessary. It was decided that they wouldn't go away for a honeymoon but would stay in Jerard's house for a week on their own, and then take both children away with them before the end of the summer; Vicki and Tony would stay with Jerard's mother for the week after the wedding.

Vicki had been overjoyed when told the news, but Tony was too young to understand what was happening, although he continued to call Jerard 'Daddy'. Sarah Daniels' reaction was one of enthusiastic approval.

'He's loved you for such a long time,' she told Velvet as they went shopping together for Velvet's wedding dress, the two children being cared for by Jerard.

Velvet frowned. 'I'm sorry,' she shook her head. 'I don't understand.'

Sarah smiled. 'I knew who you were straight away.'

'You did?' her tone was puzzled.

'Oh yes,' Sarah nodded. 'Velvet is such an unusual name. He told me all about you just after his father died.'

Velvet bit her lip; this was something she hadn't expected. 'He did?'

'You mustn't mind,' Sarah squeezed her hand. 'Jerard rarely tells me anything about his private life, so when he told me about you I knew you were very special to him. His father's death was hard on him,' she sighed. 'And then we found out Tina was ill. The poor boy was pulled two ways, between longing to go to you and between what he felt he owed Tina and Vicki. In the end he had to choose the latter—Vicki needed him desperately at the time. And so he lost you.'

'Sarah——'

'I don't blame you in the least,' the other woman assured her. 'Tina was very ill, possibly terminally, but we had no way of knowing that at the time, or that it would only be eighteen months before she died. The letter Jerard wrote to you was the hardest thing he ever had to do.'

Velvet paled. 'Letter?'

'Yes, dear. The one he wrote to you explaining his predicament—his moral obligation to Tina, his concern for Vicki as she witnessed her mother's suffering. He went through the blackest mood I've ever seen him in when he read of your marriage a few weeks later.' She shook her head. 'Still, that's all in the past,' she smiled brightly. 'You're going to be married now, and really that's all that matters, isn't it?'

'Yes,' Velvet agreed hollowly.

She knew nothing of any letter from Jerard! Not that she was likely to remember it, but surely it should still have been with her personal papers? She felt sure she would never have destroyed such a letter. So where could it be? Simon had known about the existence of Jerard, so maybe he would know about the letter too.

'All right?' Jerard kissed her lightly on the lips when she and his mother returned from their shopping trip.

He had taken to giving her these light undemonstrative kisses since the night she had agreed to marry him and they had made love so passionately.

'We got Velvet the most beautiful dress,' his mother told him.

'Is it beautiful?' His deep blue eyes probed Velvet's pale face.

She felt numb, had been this way since his mother had told her about the letter he had written to her two years ago. What had it said? Could he have made their separation sound so final that she had gone ahead and married Anthony anyway?

'It's very beautiful,' she confirmed unenthusiastically. 'It's——'

'You mustn't tell him about it, Velvet,' his mother chided. 'It's bad luck, you know.'

'Of course,' she gave a jerky smile. 'Has Tony behaved himself.'

'He always behaves!' Vicki was indignant on her soon-to-be brother's behalf.

'Not always,' Velvet smiled. 'But I take it he has today.'

Jerard was still frowning, his narrow-eyed gaze never leaving her face. 'Are you sure you're all right?' he asked her again.

She gave him a bright smile, one that didn't reach the shadows of her eyes. 'Of course.'

'Not having second thoughts?'

'No,' she shook her head firmly.

'You look pale.'

'She's tired,' his mother excused. 'We all are. A month isn't long enough to organise a wedding.'

'Is that what's wrong?' Jerard held Velvet in front of him, demanding an answer. 'Are you tired?'

'A little,' she nodded.

'Your work is nearly finished now, isn't it?'

She had kept to her decision to give up modelling. 'Nearly. Just another few days. I—Would you mind if I went home for a while? I think I'd like to lie down.'

'Lie down here,' he suggested instantly.

'No! No, I—I'd rather go home. Anyway, I have to change for this evening.' They were going out to a party; Sarah was looking after the children for the evening.

'Would you rather not go?' Jerard asked concernedly.

'I'm sure I'll be fine later.'

'Leave Tony here now,' Sarah suggested. 'That way you can have your rest in peace.'

Velvet looked at her son as he played contentedly with the toy telephone Jerard had bought him. He was so at home with these people now that she knew he wouldn't mind staying here with them. Besides, it would be easier to talk to Simon without Tony's distracting presence.

'Well, if you're sure . . .?'

'Of course,' Sarah nodded.

'I'll walk out to your car with you,' Jerard offered.

'There's no need——'

'There's every need—I don't want to kiss you in front of an audience.' The sharpness eased in his voice. 'Especially such a nosey one,' he ruffled Vicki's hair teasingly.

'I like to see you kissing Velvet,' his daughter announced happily.

'Well, you aren't going to "see" this time,' he told her firmly.

Velvet was very aware of his arm about her shoulders as they walked out to her car. In a week's time they would be man and wife. The thought made her tingle all over.

Jerard frowned, sensing her shiver. 'You aren't cold, are you?'

It was blazing sunshine. 'No,' she gave a breathless laugh. 'I—I was just thinking about the wedding.'

'Are you sure you aren't having second thoughts? I'd rather know now than on the day,' he said harshly.

'I'm just nervous, Jerard. All brides are nervous.'

'Were you this nervous when you married Anthony Dale?' he rasped.

'I don't know,' she shrugged. 'Anyway, it isn't the same, is it?'

'In what way?' His arm tightened painfully about her shoulders.

'I was younger then, probably starry-eyed——'

'Probably?' he repeated savagely. 'Don't you know?'

'You know I don't! How many times do I have to tell you that part of my life is a blank to me? What will it take to convince you?' she choked.

'You'll never convince me.' He pushed her away from him, his expression one of disgust.

'If you won't believe me, will you believe Simon?'

'Your brother?' he asked suspiciously.

'Yes, my brother. He could tell you it's the truth. Ask him! He'll tell you exactly the same thing I have.'

'It isn't that important,' Jerard dismissed harshly.

'It is to me!'

'Maybe I will ask him, one day.'

'Why not now?'

'I told you, it isn't important.'

Velvet wrenched open her car door. 'I almost hate you at times, Jerard!' She got into the car, slamming the door behind her. She didn't even spare him a second glance as she accelerated away with a screech of tyres.

It was only a short drive to her brother's house, and consequently she hadn't calmed down much by the time she arrived there. Simon appeared to be alone.

'Where's Janice?' Velvet asked abruptly.

He grinned. 'Out shopping for something to wear to your wedding. You're costing me a fortune, love. I— Hey, what is it?' He suddenly noticed her blazing eyes and flushed cheeks. 'You haven't called it off, have you?' he groaned.

'No,' she shook her head. 'Where is it, Simon?'

He frowned, completely puzzled. 'Where is what?'

Velvet sighed, some of the fight leaving her. 'The letter, Simon, where is it?'

He licked his lips, his expression suddenly guarded. 'What letter?'

'You must be terrible in court,' she scorned. 'I thought all lawyers were supposed to be deadpan?'

Simon scowled. 'Not all lawyers are confronted by a sister who's spitting fire.'

'All right, all right!' she sighed. 'I'm sorry. Jerard has just upset me and I'm taking it out on you. But I do want to see that letter. And don't go all blank on me again,' she warned. 'You're the only one who could possibly know where it is.'

Simon pursed his lips, shrugging. 'You mean the one from Jerard, don't you?'

Hope flared in her eyes. 'Then you do have it?'

'I have a letter I presume is from him,' he confirmed.

Her look was sceptical. 'You mean you've never read it?'

Simon's face flushed with anger. 'What do you think I am, a Peeping Tom?? That letter is personal, very personal, if your reaction to it at the time was anything to go by. Of course I haven't read the damned thing.'

She looked at him steadily. 'I'd like to read it now.'

'Okay,' he shrugged, standing up. 'I'll go and get it.'

When he returned several minutes later with the long white envelope and handed it to her she took out the letter with shaking fingers. Here was proof, physical proof, that she and Jerard had been in love, that they had been lovers.

It was a long letter, and she sat down to read it, missing words in her haste and having to go back over parts of it on several occasions.

It was all there, all the love and anguish his mother had said he had felt when he wrote it. His wife was very ill, in and out of hospital for check-ups, tests, anything to see if there were anything that could be done to cure her. There wasn't, and Jerard was forced to go back to living with her, to caring for her, because of Vicki mainly, but also because of Tina herself. She needed him, as she had never needed him before, and he felt honour bound to fulfil that need.

He went on to say how much he loved her, Velvet, but that if he left Tina now to take his own happiness it would destroy their love, for guilt would eat away at them both until there was nothing left of their love but bitterness.

He was right, Velvet could see that. But had she seen it then! Or had she simply married Anthony out of pique, because she couldn't have Jerard?

There were tears in her eyes as she looked up at Simon, the letter read, the letter from a man passionately in love but denied coming to her. 'Oh, Simon!' she choked, going into his waiting arms to sob on his shoulder.

'It will all work out, love,' he soothed softly. 'After all, you're going to marry Jerard now.'

Yes, she was, and she was going to make him happy if it was the last thing she ever did.

CHAPTER NINE

JERARD was slightly late calling for Velvet that evening. 'I called in to see how the children were,' he explained.

The children! It made them sound like 'theirs' already.

She pulled down her skirt as he helped her into the car, very much aware of his hard gaze on the long length of thigh that had been visible for several seconds.

'And how are they?' she asked as he got in beside her.

'Tony was already in Vicki's old cot fast asleep, and Vicki had just announced her intention of going up to keep him company,' he said dryly.

'A likely story!' she laughed.

She could look at Jerard with new eyes now, wished that he could once again be the man who had loved her so deeply he had told her to make a life without him because of his commitment to his sick wife. But that man seemed to be gone for ever, lost behind the harshness and disillusionment. And she had been the one to cause that! Maybe one day she would be able to convince him of her love—she certainly intended to try.

It was a good party, rather noisy, but everyone was in good spirits. It was the first opportunity Velvet had had to meet any of Jerard's friends. There were several covetous looks given in his direction, but one woman was particularly insistent, and finally came over to them. Jerard introduced her as Marion Walsh.

Velvet didn't like her on sight, didn't like her husky way of talking, the way she laughed and joked with Jerard about things that left Velvet completely out of the conversation. Most of all she didn't like the way the woman kept touching Jerard on the chest and arms as she talked. The truth of the matter was that she was just plain jealous!

She had a sapphire and diamond engagement ring that said Jerard belonged to her, and yet as the evening progressed and Jerard and Marion remained talking together she began to wonder whether that ring really meant anything to him, and whether a wedding ring would mean any more.

They finally left Marion Walsh to talk to some of Jerard's other friends, although as far as Velvet was concerned the whole evening had been ruined, and she found it hard to relax in Jerard's company.

'You're very quiet,' he remarked on the drive back to her flat. Tony was spending the night with Vicki.

'I'm surprised you noticed,' she said waspishly.

'I noticed,' he said grimly. 'What the hell is the matter with you?'

'Nothing!' she snapped.

'You've been in this mood all evening,' he sighed.

'Not all evening,' she corrected tautly.

'No,' he slowly agreed. 'Just since we talked to Marion.'

'*We* didn't talk to Marion,' she stared sightlessly out of the window. 'You did,' she added resentfully.

Jerard raised dark eyebrows. 'And you didn't like it?'

'No, I didn't!' Her eyes flashed as she turned to glare at him. 'Is she one of them?'

Jerard frowned. 'One of what?'

'One of those women,' she said heatedly. 'One of the select *twenty or so*.'

'What the hell are you talking about?' he asked impatiently, as he stopped the car outside her flat.

'I'm talking about you and Marion Walsh. Is she one of those twenty women you've slept with?'

Jerard looked puzzled. 'Marion is my secretary.'

'Your——? That doesn't mean you haven't slept with her,' she accused angrily. 'In fact, it's more likely that you have. Most men sleep with their secretaries.'

He reached out in the darkness and shook her. 'Will you stop that!' he ordered furiously. 'Marion is my secretary, she's never been anything else to me.'

'Oh yes?' Velvet scorned.

'Yes!' He thrust her away from him. 'But then you already knew that. Are you trying to argue with me, Velvet? Is this your way of getting out of marrying me?'

'I don't want to get out of marrying you! Why do you keep saying that?'

'Maybe I can't believe my luck.' He ran a hand through his hair.

'And maybe I can't believe mine! I didn't realise that I would be competing with your secretary. The way she kept touching you, right in front of me, was disgusting!' Velvet opened the car door and swung out on to the pavement. 'I'll be round early in the morning to pick up Tony,' and she slammed the door and walked hurriedly away.

Jerard caught up with her at her flat doorway, swinging her round to face him. 'You aren't getting rid of me that easily.' He took the key out of her hand and opened the door, pushing her inside. 'Now we are going to talk this thing out,' he told her grimly.

Velvet switched on the lights, facing him defiantly. 'There's nothing to talk out.'

'Oh yes, there is, damn you. Okay, so maybe Marion was being a little—enthusiastic——'

'Obscene is the word,' Velvet put in tautly.

His mouth quirked into a smile. 'Enthusiastic,' he insisted lightly. 'But she was only trying to get her own back. You put her nose out of joint, and she doesn't like it.'

'I'm so sorry,' her tone was sarcastic. 'Maybe *you* would prefer to call off the wedding?'

'I wasn't talking about now, Velvet,' he sighed. 'I'm talking about in Florida.'

She frowned. 'But Marion Walsh wasn't in Florida.'

'She was.'

'But I didn't see her. If she was there why didn't you get her to take care of Vicki?'

'Vicki? But—Velvet, I'm not talking about this time, I'm talking about two years ago. Marion, as my secretary, was with me that time. I'll admit that I'd decided that trip was going to make it more than a business relationship. She knew it too, which was why she was a little put out when I met and fell in love with you. We were supposed to be there working, with perhaps a little romance as well, and she didn't see me all week.' He was watching her closely, his face pale. 'You don't remember it, do you?' he said dazedly.

'No,' Velvet breathed huskily. 'I—No wonder she didn't like me just now!' She blinked back the tears. 'I didn't realise we'd met before. She must have thought me very rude.'

Jerard walked over to her as if in a trance. 'You really don't remember, do you?' he said softly.

She shook her head. 'No.'

His hands came up to cup either side of her face as he searched the bewilderment of her face. 'My God,' he choked, 'it's true. All that you told me, it's true.'

'Yes,' she nodded, biting her bottom lip.

'*God!*' He pulled her hard against him. 'You poor child!' he groaned, his face buried in her throat.

'I'm not a child, Jerard,' she cried her relief, holding him tightly to her. 'I'm so glad you believe me at last!'

'Oh, I believe you,' he said deeply, putting her away from him. 'I should have known you couldn't lie like that. Except for denying all knowledge of me you're still the girl I fell in love with, and I——'

'I am?' she asked eagerly.

'Yes,' he nodded. 'But you kept saying you didn't know me, and I thought you were ashamed of the week we'd spent together.'

Tears glistened in her deep brown eyes. 'You'll never know how much I wish I could remember it.'

'It was beautiful, Velvet. The most beautiful week I've ever spent in my life. We used to lie in bed every night watching the moonlight on the ocean—until I couldn't stop myself making love to you any longer,' he recalled huskily. 'I loved to make love to you. Each time it got better, until I was sure it couldn't be any better. But it was,' his eyes glowed. 'God, it was!'

Velvet bit her lip, frowning. 'So it was just sex with us?'

'No, it wasn't!' he shouted furiously. 'I said we made love, and that's exactly what we did. Sex is what I could have had a dozen times during the last two years, but I didn't want just a body in my bed to caress and get enjoyment from. What we had was unrepeatable, a complete joining of our minds, our souls, and lastly our bodies.'

'Are you saying there's been no one else since—since me?'

'No one,' he shook his head. 'I'd known plenty of women before you, I've already told you that, but once I'd met you, loved you, there was no one else for me.'

Velvet swallowed hard, holding her breath. 'And—and now?'

'Now?'

'How do you feel now?'

'I'm a bit dazed at the moment,' he told her ruefully. 'It seems incredible to think that the week that changed my entire life you can't even remember.'

'*I* can't remember it,' she admitted softly. 'But my

body does,' she blushed fiery red under his searching gaze. 'Every time you touch me I—I want you.' She looked up at him with apprehensive eyes.

'Oh, Velvet!' He crushed her to him. 'I wish to God you could love me.' He shook against her.

'I—I do,' she choked, tense with the enormity of her confession.

Jerard looked down at her disbelievingly. 'You do?' he probed slowly.

'Yes,' she breathed. 'I know it sounds strange, but I think if two people are supposed to love each other, then they will, no matter what barriers stand in their way. Now I can't remember knowing you the first time around, but I—I love you now . . .' She trailed off.

'You really do?' Hope lightened his voice.

'Yes,' she nodded eagerly. 'And you, how do you feel about me, now—now that you know——'

'I've never stopped loving you, Velvet, not even for a moment. I've been angry with you, impatient with you, but never out of love with you. Tell me again,' he pleaded.

'I love you. I love you!' she cried.

'She loves me!' he shouted exultantly, swinging her round in his arms, then slowly lowering her to the ground. 'I don't know if I dare kiss you,' he said shakily.

'You'd better!' Her arms went up about his neck to pull him down to her, her lips instigating the kiss, but Jerard soon took command.

This kiss was like nothing they had ever shared before, a giving and receiving of mutual love, the touching of their lips enough for both of them.

Jerard buried his face in her throat. 'I love you so much I'm burning up with it,' he admitted softly.

She caressed his cheek, the harshness gone now to be replaced by glowing love, a look of tenderness on his face that she had never seen before. 'Stay with me to-night,' she begged.

He shook his head regretfully. 'The next time I share a bed with you we'll be man and wife. I don't want you to go off and forget all about me again.'

Velvet flinched, although she knew he intended no rebuke. 'Do you hate me for marrying Anthony?' she asked guiltily.

'I told you to be happy, that your life had to go on,' he dismissed abruptly. 'I have to admit that your marriage a couple of weeks later came as something of a shock to me, but I understood.'

'Did you?' She made him look at her, seeing the raw pain in his eyes. 'Did you really?'

'No!' he cried in an agonised voice. 'I didn't understand at all. When I saw the announcement in the newspapers I contemplated suicide——'

'Oh no!' she gasped. 'Not you, Jerard,' she shook her head dazedly. 'You're too strong to do something like that.'

'Believe me, it was only the thought of leaving Vicki with a very sick mother that stopped me,' he revealed harshly. 'I couldn't do that to her—or Tina. Then about six months later I saw the report of your plane crash,' he sighed.

'Anthony had only just got his licence.' Velvet had been allowed to read the newspaper reports too, mainly in the hope that it might jog a memory. It hadn't. 'It was the first time he'd taken up a passenger.'

'He was a bloody fool, taking you in your condition,' Jerard rasped.

'They said it was the trauma of Anthony's death that caused the shock and Tony's premature birth,' she recalled dully, 'not the crash itself.'

'He still had no business—What the hell, the man's dead now,' he shrugged off his anger towards Anthony.

'I wanted to come and see you, but Tina was even worse by then, her illness was becoming critical, and our situation would still have been the same, I was still tied to her. I did call the hospital, though, and they said that both you and the baby were well.'

'Tony was in an incubator for a while, but only because he was so small, not because he was ill.'

'It was obvious by this time that Tina wasn't going to make it, but I couldn't let you know that, it would have been as if I were wishing her to die,' he revealed abruptly. 'Even if my divorce from Tina had gone through as it should have done I would still have felt tied to her when I found out how ill she was.'

'You were divorcing her?'

'Of course, you wouldn't remember that either. When I met you my divorce was going through the final stages. I had to leave Florida in a hurry because of my father's sudden death, and it was while we were standing at his graveside that Tina chose to tell me of her serious heart condition. I thought the whole damn world was falling in about my head,' he groaned.

'You poor darling,' she choked, wanting to be closer to him. 'You must have hated me when I married Anthony.'

'I didn't hate you—I've never hated you. I hated the circumstances that made it impossible for me to marry you. And I'd already stolen a week of your life, I couldn't ask you to accept anything less than marriage from me, not when it looked as if Tina would just be very weak, possibly bedridden, for many years to come. But it doesn't matter now,' he smiled. 'We love each other, and we're going to be married, that's all that does, or can, matter to us now. The past is over.'

There was so much love in his face that she felt like crying. 'Kiss me,' she pleaded.

'Gladly,' he breathed against her mouth, parting her

lips in a long and hungry kiss. 'This won't do,' he said briskly. 'All my good intentions will fly out of the window if I stay here much longer.'

'I wish they would.' She clung to him. 'Please, Jerard!'

'No,' his tone was firm. 'I'm not proud of the fact that I took advantage of your love last time——'

'It wasn't taking advantage if we both wanted it!'

'I was older than you, and I wasn't free. I should have had more control. But after I'd loved you the first time I didn't want to spend a minute away from you.'

'That's how I feel now,' she pouted.

He smiled, kissing her gently on the lips. 'We have the rest of our lives together this time, let's not spoil it.'

She knew he was right, but it didn't make parting from him any easier. She kissed him goodnight with so much longing that he almost relented, although he finally managed to put her away from him.

'One week,' he murmured against her mouth. 'One more week and you'll be mine.' His arms tightened about her. 'You'll be Mrs Jerard Daniels.'

'Oh, Jerard!' she said shakily.

'I love Tony, you know,' he told her huskily. 'I don't want there ever to be any doubt about that.'

'There isn't.' She had seen him with her son enough to know of his real affection for him. 'And I love Vicki too.'

Jerard grinned at her. 'So it's all nice and tidy.'

'Our love isn't *tidy*,' she chided. 'I find it breathtaking.'

'So do I.' Against he kissed her. 'I'll find it even more breathtaking when you're my wife, I'll have to keep pinching myself to make sure it's true. I have to go now, Velvet. But I'll see you tomorrow?'

'Try and stop me,' she said eagerly.

'I never want you to stop, Velvet,' he told her

seriously, his gaze holding hers mesmerised. 'These last few weeks when I thought I'd lost your love for ever have been hell for me.'

'Me too,' she blushed.

'In a week's time we'll never be parted again. It's going to be the longest week of my life.'

There were so many last-minute plans to take care of that contrary to Jerard's belief the time simply rushed by. So much so that by the Friday she was just relieved that they only had to meet her parents, her brother and his family from the airport, all of whom had decided to come for the wedding.

Simon came to the airport too, taking Nigel, Jenny and the children back in his car, leaving her parents to ride with Jerard and herself. He was an instant hit, she could tell that, charming her mother until she blushed prettily and impressing her father with his business capabilities.

She knew her parents were concerned about the short time she and Jerard had apparently known each other, and she hastened to reassure her mother as she helped her unpack once they reached her flat. Her parents, brother and his family were taking over her flat for a couple of weeks, and while it was going to be very crowded tonight it should be a little easier once she and Tony had moved out tomorrow.

'He's fascinating, Velvet,' her mother gave an approving smile. 'And he has such a charming little girl.'

And Vicki was charming; the tantrums had totally stopped, and there was a new confidence about her. She had been so excited about the prospect of meeting a new grandmother, a new uncle and aunt, and her two cousins. And she and Tony were inseparable, something that caused Jerard and Velvet great amusement. Jerard had joked about what a good older sister she was going to make to any other children they had too. It had never occurred to Velvet that she and Jerard would have children together, and just the thought of it gave her a warm glow. She felt it would also show Vicki that not all things bad happened at hospitals.

'And he's marvellous with Tony,' her mother added enthusiastically.

'I gather you like him,' she teased.

'He's wonderful, Velvet. Your father and I can see how much in love you both are.' She squeezed her hand. 'We so want to see you happy again.'

'I am.' She blinked back the tears.

'Then that's all your father and I wanted to know.'

'Hey, this is going to be a wedding,' Jerard said softly from the doorway. 'And I won't allow anyone to cry at our wedding,' he told them.

'We're just happy, darling,' Velvet told him as she went to join him, her happiness now complete with her parents' approval.

Their wedding day dawned bright and sunny, the ceremony was simple but beautiful. Jerard looked so handsome, his eyes never leaving her face as he solemnly made his vows to her, the love and sincerity in his voice telling her that he meant every word.

'You see,' Carly was telling Paul as Velvet joined them at the small reception they were holding at Jerard's mother's house, 'there's nothing to it.'

'To what?' she smiled at them.

'I'm trying to persuade him that getting married isn't so bad,' Carly explained ruefully. 'So far I'm not making much headway.'

'Maybe because you haven't let me get a word in edgeways,' Paul drawled. 'If you had you might have heard me agree.'

'His girl-friend gasped. 'I—I might?'

'Definitely,' he nodded.

'Really?'

He raised his eyebrows heavenwards. 'What does it take to convince you?'

'A wedding!'

'Well?' Velvet challenged Paul.

He shrugged. 'Suits me.'

'I was a witness to that, Carly,' she grinned.

Jerard appeared at her side, his arm going possessively about her waist. 'Time we were leaving, darling,' he told her deeply.

Now that the time had come for them to be alone together she felt so nervous she shook with it. Not that she was in the least afraid of Jerard, or of being married to him, but as far as she was concerned this would be her first night with any man, the Jerard of the past and being married to Anthony all a blank to her, and she felt as nervous as any young virgin bride, despite being a mother to Tony.

Their goodbyes were tearful, almost as if they were going to another country, and not just a couple of miles down the road.

'All right?' he asked once they had managed to get away from the two tearful mothers.

'Fine,' she answered breathlessly.

'Nervous?'

'A little,' she admitted, swallowing hard.

His hand came out to entwine with hers while he drove. 'You needn't be. I'm not going to suddenly turn into a sex maniac when we get home.'

'I know that,' she smiled at his teasing. 'It's just that— well, I——'

'I know, darling,' he squeezed her hand reassuringly.

And she knew that he did know, that he realised her nervousness was due to her inexperience—and she loved him all the more for it. It would be all right, everything would be all right, Jerard would see to that.

'We're going to have a nice quiet dinner for two,' he

continued. 'Which we will prepare for ourselves. I've given my—our housekeeper the week off, so I hope you don't mind helping with the cooking and cleaning?'

'I'll love it!' Her eyes glowed.

'So will I,' he said gruffly. 'After dinner we're going to listen to a few romantic records, dance a little, and then I'm going to seduce you on the carpet.'

'Jerard!' she blushed.

He gave a husky laugh of enjoyment. 'Don't you like my programme for the evening?'

'Too much!'

'*You're* too much,' he told her throatily. 'I hope I can wait until after dinner,' he groaned.

He did, just. He was a considerate lover, raised her to the heights time and time again before taking them both over the edge of sensual excitement into ecstatic pleasure. It seemed to Velvet that she must have fainted for a moment, only to come awake in Jerard's arms, her body still joined to his, lethargic with pleasure, a drowsy pleasure that made it difficult for her to open her eyes.

'Velvet?' Jerard moved to look down at her, leaning on his elbow, his eyes half-closed with newly aroused passion.

'Mm?' she reached up for him, their lips meeting in a clinging kiss.

'You see how it is with us?' he murmured against her throat. 'And it will get better and better, you'll see.'

'Better than that?' At last her eyes opened.

'You'll see,' he promised. 'In the meantime we're going to take a shower together.'

Her hands clung about his neck as he swung her up against him. 'Have we showered together before?'

'Lots of times,' he nodded.

She smiled happily. 'It sounds fun.'

He gave a contented laugh. 'I love you, Velvet.'

'And I love you,' she told him seriously.

She lay beside Jerard, numb, unable to feel the cramp in the leg he had trapped beneath his.

He was going to hate her when he knew the truth. *If it were the truth!* But it had to be, *it had to be!*

She had to get out of here, leave before Jerard woke up and saw the state she was in and demanded an explanation. And she couldn't possibly tell him, not yet.

She moved slowly about the bedroom pulling on her clothes. Jerard was in a very deep sleep after their love-making. She didn't even know where she was going, just away from here, before Jerard learnt to hate her.

She walked for hours, slowly making her way to Simon's as it started to become light. He wouldn't thank her for waking him at this early hour, although once he saw her he might be forgiving.

To her surprise he was already up and dressed, but unshaven, a haggard look to his features. He didn't say a word as he led her into the house, and neither did Janice as she put the cup of hot coffee in front of her.

'Jerard was here,' she guessed dully.

'Yes,' Simon nodded. 'He's out of his mind with worry, Velvet.' Her brother stood up. 'I'd better call him, tell him——'

'No!' The cup landed on its saucer with a clatter. 'I don't want you to call him. I—I can't see him just yet.'

'But what's he done, Velvet?' Simon frowned worriedly.

'It isn't what Jerard's done, it's what I've done. At least, what I think I've done.'

Simon shook his head. 'You aren't making much sense, love,' he told her gently.

'I—It was the shock,' she said dazedly. 'The shock of—of——'

'Yes?' he prompted.

She licked her lips, giving a choked sob. 'Just tell me one thing, Simon. Was I pregnant when I married Anthony?'

CHAPTER TEN

SIMON seemed to pale, turning away. 'I—What makes you think that?' he asked at last.

'Nothing makes me *think* it,' Velvet said shrilly. 'It's the truth, isn't it?'

He sighed. 'How did you find out?'

'My God,' she shook with reaction, 'it is true! And the baby was Jerard's!' The world about her suddenly seemed to fade and go black.

She woke up to find herself lying on Simon's sofa, struggling to sit up as it all came back to her, the realisation that Jerard was Tony's father! She buried her face in her hands, sobbing uncontrollably.

Simon's arm came about her shoulders as he sat down next to her, pulling her against him as he tried to comfort her. 'It's all right,' he soothed. 'It's all right, Velvet.'

'Of course it isn't!' She moved back, her cheeks tear-wet. 'Jerard's going to hate me when he knows.'

'He may not find out——'

'I'm going to tell him,' she said firmly. 'As soon as I feel strong enough I'm going back to the house and tell him. But first I need you to tell me exactly what happened. Why did Anthony marry me?' she choked.

Simon shrugged. 'Beccause he loved you.'

'Even though I was pregnant by another man!'

'Yes,' her brother nodded. 'How did you find out, Velvet?' he asked again.

'Tony—Tony has a birthmark on his left thigh.'

'Yes, I've seen it.'

She blushed. 'Jerard has one exactly like it.'

'Oh.'

'It was too much of a coincidence, considering our past relationship,' she cried her distress. 'It's exactly the same—same place, same shape. And it had been puzzling me why I would marry Anthony when I was apparently so much in love with Jerard. I thought I loved Anthony, but I must have been completely in love with Jerard to have acted the way I did with him.'

'Yes,' Simon sighed. 'You broke off your engagement to Anthony as soon as you got back from Florida that first time. You were completely honest about the whole thing, and you said you would be marrying once Jerard got his divorce. Then that letter arrived,' he sighed heavily. 'And about the same time you realised you were pregnant. Anthony still wanted to marry you, and so——'

'And so I took advantage of that love and married him!' she finished disgustedly. 'Because I was too much of a coward——'

'No!' her brother's voice was sharp. 'You wanted to bring the baby up on your own. I'm afraid it was the pressure Anthony and I put on you that finally made you give in.'

'I don't believe——'

'It's the truth,' Simon rasped. 'At the time I thought I was doing the right thing by persuading you to marry Anthony. No matter what they tell you about illegitimacy being accepted nowadays, there's still a stigma attached to it. But I don't think you and Anthony were ever husband and wife in the true sense of a marriage.'

'You don't *think*?' Velvet exploded.

'All right, I know you weren't,' he sighed. 'You were still in love with Jerard, and then there was your pregnancy.'

'Just how premature was Tony?' she asked shrewdly.

'Six weeks,' he muttered.

'And not the three months I thought.' Her mouth twisted.

Simon drew in a deep breath. 'When you came back from Florida this time and said you'd met Jerard again, and that he was free, I couldn't believe it.'

'Do you have any idea what he's going to do when he finds out what I've done?' she choked. 'He's going to hate me.'

'No——'

'Yes!' She glared at him. 'I gave his son another man as his father. Jerard loves me now, but once he knows the truth he'll hate me. And he'll take Tony away from me,' her voice broke emotionally.

'He wouldn't——'

'Wouldn't you?' she demanded tautly. 'Put yourself in his place. He loved me, and yet because his wife was seriously ill he had to stand by her and his daughter. And because I was pregnant by him I married someone else, I denied him all knowledge of the child we'd made together. Yesterday I was the happiest girl in the world, today—today, I feel in the depths of hell!'

Simon's expression was agonised. 'I had no idea his wife was ill—you never told us that, only that he could never marry you. I thought—I assumed he'd taken his fun and was now backing out of the relationship.'

'You've had that letter for two years now, Simon, maybe you should have read it, or maybe I should have shown you it in the first place. Jerard didn't want to give me up—he had to.'

'I didn't know,' he groaned. 'None of us did.'

'No,' she agreed heavily. 'And I have no one else to blame but myself for marrying Anthony, my own cowardice in telling the world I'd loved a man without being married to him. I was a stupid little fool.'

'It seemed as if everything was going to work out okay when you said you were going to marry Jerard this time,' Simon said dully.

'Yes. But didn't you think I should be told he was Tony's father before I married him?' Velvet asked in exasperation. 'He had a right to be told.'

Simon sighed. 'I just didn't know what to do for the best.' He shrugged. 'Jerard was going to be Tony's father anyway——'

'He *is* his father,' she cut in firmly. 'I'm going to see Tony now, it might be the last opportunity I have to be with him.'

'Velvet——'

'Don't say any more, Simon,' she shook her head sadly. 'I realise that it was ultimately my decision to marry Anthony, even if it was the wrong one. But you should have told me.' She moved to kiss Janice on the cheek.

'Don't go like this, Velvet,' her sister-in-law pleaded. 'Stay and we'll talk——'

'It's much too late for talking,' Velvet said dully. 'I must go now. I—I'll call you.'

She took a taxi to Jerard's mother's house, as her car was still at the flat; her parents were using it for their visit. Sarah was up too, and looked as if she had been for hours.

'Velvet!' she exclaimed her relief. 'Oh, I'm so glad you're here, my dear,' and she hugged her.

'Jerard?' Velvet asked apprehensively, frightened he was still here.

'Been and gone, back to the house, I think.' Sarah frowned. 'I don't know what my son has done——'

'Nothing,' Velvet choked. 'He's done nothing.'

'He seemed to think he must have done,' Sarah said gently.

'No,' she shook her head.

'But he woke up in the night and you'd gone!'

She swallowed hard. 'I've never meant to hurt Jerard,

Sarah,' she looked at her mother-in-law pleadingly. 'Please believe me when I say I love him above life itself.'

'I know that, my dear,' Sarah nodded. 'And he loves you in the same way. He's ill with worry about you,' she added searchingly.

Velvet sat down abruptly, feeling ill herself. 'I've done him a terrible wrong. I've done something so bad——'

'Nothing you do could be so bad he won't forgive you. He loves you so much, Velvet,' she told her softly. 'For two years I watched him suffer with loving you, watched him die a little each day. The change in him after meeting you again is enough to tell me that nothing you do will ever kill that love.'

'But I've denied him his son!' came Velvet's anguished cry.

Sarah was silent, although her bottom lip trembled emotionally. Velvet looked at her searchingly, tears streaming down her cheeks.

'Did you hear what I said?' she choked as Sarah said nothing.

'Yes,' Sarah nodded.

'Well?'

Sarah seemed to be choosing her words with care. 'You're talking of Tony, of course?'

'Yes!'

Sarah nodded. 'I thought so.'

Velvet frowned at her calm attitude. 'You don't seem—surprised?'

'I'm not. Oh, my dear, I already knew!'

'You did?' she gasped.

'Of course.'

'But I—How?' It couldn't be because of any facial likeness to Jerard, Tony looked nothing like him.

'I've bathed him, Velvet,' Sarah explained gently. 'All the Daniels men have that birthmark. I would have been a fool not to know Tony was my own grandchild.'

'And you don't hate me?' Velvet's eyes were wide.

Sarah's expression was one of understanding, not one of condemnation. 'I couldn't possibly hate the woman who has given my son so much happiness.'

Velvet shook her head. 'Denying him Tony wasn't giving him happiness. Could I—could I see Tony now?'

'Of course. He and Vicki are already up and playing in the nursery.'

They both stood up, and Velvet ran into the other woman's arms. 'I'm sorry,' she cried. 'So very sorry.'

'You have nothing to be sorry about,' her mother-in-law soothed. 'But I think you should give Jerard the chance to show you that it doesn't change anything between you.'

'I can't,' she shuddered, envisaging Jerard's cold anger when he was told Tony was his son. 'Not yet.'

'Go and see the children now,' Sarah encouraged. 'Spend some time with them. You'll see, children have a way of making the oddest things seem normal.'

Velvet gave a watery smile. 'Not this,' she shook her head, leaving the room to be with Vicki and Tony.

Both the children had just got out of bed, Tony looking adorable in his pyjamas, Vicki looking pretty in her flowered cotton nightdress. There were toys everywhere, and once the first ecstatic greeting was over Velvet sat down on the floor to play with them.

She had no idea when Jerard entered the room, wasn't aware of his presence until Vicki called out excitedly, running over to launch herself into her father's arms. Tony ran to him too, his arms clutching about his legs as he gazed up adoringly.

Velvet slowly raised her eyes to meet Jerard's searching gaze, paling as she saw how ill he looked, his face suddenly gaunt, pain in his eyes that he made no effort to hide.

'Your mother called you,' she guessed jerkily, slowly getting to her feet, running sweaty palms down her denim-clad thighs.

'Yes,' his voice was husky with emotion. 'Why, Velvet?' he asked abruptly.

'I—Your mother didn't tell you?'

'No,' he shook his head. 'You tell me.'

His gaze was mesmerising in its intensity, and Velvet felt her breath constrict in her throat. God, she loved this man!

'Tell you what, Daddy?' Vicki wanted to know.

He smiled down at his daughter, and only Velvet was able to tell the strain it was to him. 'Grandma's waiting for you to go down and have breakfast with her.'

'Oh, goody!' Vicki struggled to go down. 'Tony too?'

'No,' Velvet's tone was sharper than she intended. 'Not yet, Vicki,' she smiled to take the sting out of her words. 'I—Daddy will bring him down in a moment.'

'Okay,' Vicki shrugged, food being paramount in her list of priorities at the moment.

'Why, Velvet?' Jerard repeated once his daughter had left the room.

She couldn't tell him! She couldn't destroy the love radiating from every pore of his body; she wanted to bask in that love, forget the rest of the world in Jerard's all-consuming possession.

'Shall I help you?' his voice was harsh. 'You didn't love me after all? It was all a mistake?'

'No!' she cried. 'Oh no, Jerard, nothing like that.'

'Then what?' He bent to pick Tony up as the little boy kept pulling on his trousers. 'What the hell was so serious you had to run out on me in the middle of the night?'

'I don't even know where to start.' She turned away.

'The beginning is usually the best place,' he drawled.

She shrugged. 'There is no beginning, only an end.'

'Then tell me the end!' he rasped. 'But for God's sake tell me *something.*' He was charged with a leashed tension. 'Is there something you haven't told me, is that it?'

'Yes. Yes!'

'Then tell me now,' he ordered. 'Maybe it won't be the shock you think it is.'

Velvet looked at him searchingly. 'Maybe you should sit down. Maybe——'

'I'm not so old that I can't take whatever it is you have to tell me while standing on my own two feet. Hey, stop that,' he chided Tony gently, taking his hand out of his open shirt. 'Don't pull Daddy's hairs,' he teased, tickling the little boy until he giggled.

Velvet's heart constricted in her chest. They looked so natural together, so—so right. She moved to snatch her son out of Jerard's arms, holding him possessively to her. She couldn't give Tony up, she just couldn't!

'So that's it,' Jerard said softly, his eyes narrowed.

'That's what?' she queried sharply.

'He's yours, Velvet,' he told her gently. 'All yours.'

She frowned. 'What do you mean?'

Jerard sighed. 'I mean the identical birthmarks.'

She gasped, almost dropping Tony in her shock. 'You—you know?'

'Yes, I know.'

'Since— when?' she asked dazedly.

'Since I looked after Tony a couple of days ago. You'd gone shopping with my mother and Vicki. Tony tipped orange juice all over himself, and I had to change his clothes.' He shrugged. 'I saw it then.'

'And you said *nothing*?'

'What could I say?' he exploded savagely. 'Oh, I'll admit I was in shock for a couple of hours, but I worked it out that you didn't know either. You would have told me if you had known.'

She swallowed hard, finding it hard to take this in.

'You—you married me anyway, even knowing Tony was your son? Or was that the reason you did marry me?' she demanded to know. 'Is that the reason——'

'If you say one more word I swear I'll kiss you sense-less—even in front of our son,' he told her, dangerously soft so as not to alarm Tony. 'I wanted to marry you before I knew about Tony, when I thought he was an-other man's child. I can't deny that I was ecstatic when I found out he was mine, but it made no difference to the desperation with which I wanted to make you my wife. You know how intensely I've wanted you, how much I need you. If I had to give up everything, includ-ing Vicki and Tony, I would do it, for you.'

'But I even named your son after another man,' she sobbed.

'I'm proud that he bears that name,' Jerard said huskily. 'He must have been quite a man, taking on the responsibility of another man's child.' He took Tony out of her arms, putting him down on the floor and interesting him in a toy tractor. Then he stood up to pull Velvet roughly into his arms. 'I love you, you stupid woman,' he groaned. 'One day, when Tony is old enough to understand a love as strong as ours, we'll tell him the true facts about his birth. He'll love you almost as much as I do.'

'Oh, Jerard, I love you too!' she sobbed against him, feeling as if her life had just been given back to her.

He kissed her briefly. 'Now let's take Tony and join my mother and Vicki for breakfast. And then we're going home to continue our honeymoon—and we aren't coming out for a week!' He picked up his son, his arm about Velvet's waist as they all went downstairs to-gether.

The bestselling epic saga of the Irish. An intriguing and passionate story that spans 400 years.

FIRST...

The Defiant

Lady Elizabeth Hatton, highborn Englishwoman, was not above using her position to get what she wanted ...and more than anything in the world she wanted Rory O'Donnell, the fiery Irish rebel. But it was an alliance that promised only ruin....

THEN...

The Survivors

Against a turbulent background of political intrigue and royal corruption, the determined, passionate Shanna O'Hara searched for peace in her beloved but troubled Ireland. Meanwhile in England, hot-tempered Brenna Coke fought against a loveless marriage....

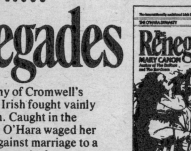

Experience the warmth of …

Harlequin Romance

Delightful and intriguing love stories
by the world's foremost writers
of romance fiction.

Be whisked away to dazzling
international capitals …
or quaint European villages.
Experience the joys of falling in love …
for the first time, the best time!

Harlequin Romance

A uniquely absorbing journey into a world of superb romance reading.

No one touches the heart of a woman quite like Harlequin!

Take these
4 best-selling
novels
FREE

Yes! Four sophisticated,
contemporary love stories
by four world-famous
authors of romance
FREE, as your
introduction to the Harlequin Presents
subscription plan. Thrill to **Anne Mather**'s
passionate story BORN OUT OF LOVE, set
in the Caribbean.... Travel to darkest Africa
in **Violet Winspear**'s TIME OF THE TEMPTRESS....Let
Charlotte Lamb take you to the fascinating world of London's
Fleet Street in MAN'S WORLD ....Discover beautiful Greece in
Sally Wentworth's moving romance SAY HELLO TO YESTERDAY.

Harlequin
Presents...

*The very finest
in romance fiction*

Join the millions of avid Harlequin readers all over the
world who delight in the magic of a really exciting novel.
EIGHT great NEW titles published EACH MONTH!
Each month you will get to know exciting, interesting,
true-to-life people .... You'll be swept to distant lands you've
dreamed of visiting .... Intrigue, adventure, romance, and
the destiny of many lives will thrill you through each
Harlequin Presents novel.

Get all the latest books before they're sold out!
As a Harlequin subscriber you actually receive your
personal copies of the latest Presents novels immediately
after they come off the press, so you're sure of getting all
8 each month.

Cancel your subscription whenever you wish!
You don't have to buy any minimum number of books.
Whenever you decide to stop your subscription just let us
now and we'll cancel all further shipments.